Dear

So great
seeing you
again! Yay!
Sing on!
& enjoy the
book

Sophie
Glass

I'VE KNOWN SINCE I WAS EIGHT

I'VE KNOWN SINCE I WAS EIGHT

Sophie Glasser

iUniverse, Inc.
New York Lincoln Shanghai

I've Known Since I Was Eight

iUniverse, Inc.

For information address:
iUniverse, Inc.
2021 Pine Lake Road, Suite 100
Lincoln, NE 68512
www.iuniverse.com

ISBN: 0-595-29333-6

Printed in the United States of America

For my parents, for supporting me and believing in me, and for R.H.K., my wonderful partner.

Acknowledgements

Dozens of people helped me to get this book in final form, and to all them, a heart filled thank you:

My success team, who helped me finally get the manuscript together: Gwen Acton, Nancy Schiff, Beth Mozell, Robert Pierson, Bob Myers, David Barnes, and Jim Wadleigh; Eva Schlesinger, my friend who confirmed my love of reading and writing young adult literature; the Society of Children's Book Writers and Illustrators; the Massachusetts Audubon Society; Mizuko Akiba, the woman I met on the subway who grew up in Ithaca and helped me with details; my long-term Boston friends Robin Goldstein, Shana Holland, Hena Susha Schiffman, and Laura Harrington for being there; Trish Keohain for reminding me to be gentle with myself; Nancy Lee Sayre for reminding me about humor; Richard Goldberg for being my "perm" buddy while working temporary jobs; Jennifer Moore for being a great spiritual mentor; my late friend Susan Pompkin for supporting the organic process; Kerry Mullen for letting me use her computer to type up my earliest draft; the former Crone's Harvest bookstore in Jamaica Plain, MA "Women Reading What We've Written" open reading series, where I first read chapter 17; David Zuckerman, for helping me to remember that men are good (and that bald-headedness is beautiful); Emily Fenster and the women of the lesbian rap group in Cambridge, Massachusetts; Jennifer Keith Little for loving my book: Madeline McNeeley for cheering me on; Julia Chu, Cyn Green, Patty Harney, and Lois Presser for good times with the girls at Cornell; Sharon Weisberger for being my E.A.R.S. buddy; my C.H.U.D. group at Cornell, especially Ern Otani and Wendy Wagner; Ken Zirkel for the author photo and for the wonderful cover; Pam Moline and Erika Phillips for last minute edits; Paula Kravitz for grammatical advice; the town of Ithaca for being its wonderful self; Professor Biddy Martin and the Cornell "Introduction to Women Studies" class of Fall, 1985, for helping me realize it's okay to be gay; Sarah Duncan and Lynn Rosenbaum for rooting for me; the staff of the Lesley University 4th floor computer lab for computer help; Jon McWilliams of iuniverse.com for being so patient with my questions; my parents for their love and support; Batsy Bomb for lots of meows and cuddles; and R.H.K. for love and affection.

CHAPTER 1

"Isn't he gorgeous?" Freida said, pointing at the magazine model.

"Yeah," agreed Sylvia, munching on her sandwich. "He's *really* hot. What do you think, Sarah?"

"Yeah, yeah, he's cute," I said, trying to sound convincing. I'd rather have been looking at the female models, but I'd rather have died than said it.

"So does anyone have a date yet for the Junior dance?" Libby said, redoing her makeup at the table.

"I do," I piped up, relieved. "Jarod and I said we'd be each other's date. We're just friends of course, but anyway, he's my date."

"Really?" said Sylvia. "I'm still hoping Wendell will ask me, and I definitely am not just interested in being platonic friends. But since we're all going as a group, I'm not going to worry about being asked."

"Me either," said Freida, brushing out her long blond curls. "Well, at least you have Jarod, Sarah. You two are together so much it just makes sense, and who knows? Maybe you'll change your mind and go for him." She winked at me. My boy crazy friend Freida, she really meant well. I jokingly slugged her on the arm.

I knew Jarod and I looked like a cute couple. I'd often noticed Jarod's long brown hair tied back in a ponytail, similar to my long curly brown hair. At five feet four inches, I was just a bit shorter than him. We did look good together, but the truth was we were just friends.

Jarod was the only person who knew about me being gay. I felt petrified that if the girls knew, even Freida, who I was closest with, that they'd dump me as their friend or something. But I was glad I could at least tell Jarod.

He and I had hung out since he moved here to Ithaca five years ago. We could tell each other anything, and he was real non-sexist, too, with a lot of female friends. He was even bisexual! He had told me about a crush he had on a guy a few years ago, and Jarod didn't even seem to worry about it like I did. Probably that was because one of his older brothers was gay (!), and his family was into politically correct stuff and seemed okay with it. Still, it helped me feel better to know someone else who wasn't totally straight.

And with him as my "date" at the dance next month, I wouldn't have to deal with questions from the others about who I was going to ask or anything. Plus we were going with a bunch of our friends, so I knew it would be fun. Still, though, being in the eleventh grade and being gay sometimes felt like a death sentence, because I was always worrying about how people would react if they knew. Aside from that, though, I felt good about being gay; after all, I was who I was, and I looked forward to a time when I wouldn't feel I had to hide it.

I've known since I was eight. Whenever the other girls would say that certain guys were cute, or they liked to look at male models in the fashion magazines or *Playgirl*, it never interested *me*. I thought the female models were cute, or that my friends were! But mostly I'd get crushed out on the college-age sisters of some friends, women science teachers, or on girls I didn't know, like in the other classes.

If I could really ask anyone to the dance, I knew I'd ask Tina Hawkins. She was in my economics class and sat the next row over. We chatted sometimes, and sometimes she seemed to be looking at me so openly, it made me wonder: Did she like me? Or could she tell I was a lesbian? Mostly I doubted it but just stared at the side of her head and her short blond hair and told myself to forget it.

Being gay and worrying what other people might think scared me to death, but I guessed I'd have to face it eventually. After all, I'd known since I was eight, and it was bound to come out into the open sometime.

CHAPTER 2

"Want to meet by the waterfall?" asked Jarod over the phone.

"Great. Half-hour?"

"Half-hour."

It was a beautiful day, and I was psyched to get outside. Meeting by the waterfall in the gorge was one of Jarod's and my favorite things to do. Most of the other high school kids prefer the reservoir, but I like the quietness and privacy of the gorges. They're so spectacular-looking, too.

I grabbed a purple towel and my suntan lotion and strode outside. It was definitely a gorgeous day, great for sunbathing.

As I walked the half-mile to the gorge, I thought more about Tina Hawkins. Now we would really make a cute couple, I thought. Her short blond hair, cut just past her ears, and her bright blue eyes were a nice contrast to my long curly brown hair and brown eyes. She was a little shorter than me, too, and I could just picture putting my arm around her and stroking her shoulder. I wondered what she thought about, and if I could ever have her as a girlfriend. Then I thought to myself: be real, that's asking too much. I'd have to content myself with watching her in class or sneaking a look at her dancing. And what were the chances she'd be gay?

Just then, a boy and a girl rounded the corner, holding hands and laughing and joking. I wanted to throw up.

Pushing it out of my mind, I watched some birds in a tree nearby, trying to recognize what kind they were. The bluejays of summer, it looked like. Looking at birds always calmed me down, and already I was breathing easier. I whistled my way over to the falls, where Jarod was already sunbathing.

"Hey, sport!" he called, staying in his face-down tanning position. "You're pokey today."

"I know, I know. Just daydreaming, I guess."

"Pull up a rock."

"Coming right up." I picked up a little stone and pretended to be a waitress. "Here's your order, sir," and I laid it next to his head.

"Thank you very much, ma'am." He pushed his long brown hair away from his face and smiled.

I spread out my towel next to his. We've been coming here every warm weekend for the past two or three years. It's nice to be older now so that our parents don't give us such a hassle. Until ninth grade, they always insisted that one of them come with us. We didn't know if it was because we were so young or because they thought we'd sneak off and have sex or something. In any case, they've relaxed now and they seem to realize we really are just friends.

I met Jarod when we both had paper routes for the local paper. We'd pick up our papers early in the morning, around six a.m., and then we'd give each other knowing glances when we'd be struggling to stay awake in the boring afternoon classed like Mr. MacNamara's history or Ms. Fidro's math. Then some days when the papers were late arriving at the pickup point, we'd chat and after a while we just started hanging out more and became good friends.

And somehow we both knew and understood that we both just wanted to be friends, so that made things really comfortable. Jarod had always seemed real down-to-earth and straightforward, not into game-playing or flirting like a lot of other guys. And maybe his long hair helped me feel more comfortable, too, because he didn't try to look "masculine" in that way like most other boys.

He'd mentioned to me early on about his crush on Louis, his friend from camp, and he didn't act embarrassed about it at all. So of course that had made it easier to tell him all about my crushes.

Later, Jarod had said he guessed I was gay before that because I didn't flirt with him and didn't talk about other guys I liked. He also just felt like my "energy" wasn't into checking out guys, and so he had just guessed. That freaked me out because I worried that other kids would guess I was gay, too, Jarod had said no, though, that they can only know if they're attuned to that sort of thing. Since his older brother is gay and since he himself is bi, Jarod felt more attuned than most people to gayness and says he has "Gaydar." Even then, he'd added, he might not have noticed it in me if we hadn't known each other so well. Anyway, it had definitely been a relief to hear that he didn't think others could tell.

We lay out in the sun and chatted.

"So what ya been up to?" he asked.

"Not much. Just trying not to obsess about my lonely heart." I put a tad of sun block on my nose. "You?"

"Well, I went shopping with Abdul for a suit. It took us a few hours of combing the mall and trying on twenty suits, but I think I found a good one."

"Really? What's it like?"

"Oh, it's a dark blue, and depending on the ties, it can be casual or dressy. It feels a bit stuffy, but that's how suits are, I guess. It's nice to feel so adult in it, though."

"Yeah, that makes sense."

"What about you? Did you find a new dress yet?"

"No, I'll probably go next week or something. My mom's giving me a hassle about what color and style I should get. I want something purple, so we'll see."

"I'm sure you'll find something great. And I can't wait to ride in that limo!"

"Yeah, me too." The whole bunch of us were renting a limo to go to the prom in together: me, Jarod, Freida, Abdul, Gus, Wendell, Sylvia, Tommy, and Libby. Plus I wasn't getting my hopes up at all, but Freida was getting friendly with Tina, and Freida mentioned she'd ask if Tina or a few other girls wanted to come with us. That would be heaven! But I reminded myself that it was ridiculous to think that anything might happen with me and Tina. Still, I knew I'd love it if Tina came with us.

"So, Jarod, do you know yet if she's joining us?" I raised my eyebrows at him so he'd know who I meant. He already knew all about my crush, of course.

"I don't know but I still think she might. Tina doesn't seem as close to Mindy, Brenda, and Helen anymore, so it seems like there's a good chance. I hope she does for your sake."

I sat up. "Yeah, but then again, what good is it? She's probably straight."

"You never know. I can't *quite* figure her energy out. I think there's a possibility…" Jarod's always talking about people's energies.

"You're just saying that!"

"No, I'm not, really. She could be. I mean, she might be gay, who knows? Just try to get to know her, be casual."

I lay back down and tried to get comfortable on my rock. "Yeah, yeah, you're right. Somewhere there's another person in this 10%."

"That's right. And I'm in the 5%—I have a crush on both Libby *and* Gus. I'm just waiting to see which one seems more promising. You should just wait and see, too, and try not to worry."

"Yeah. You're right. I need to RELAX!"

"Mmm." He turned over on his back. "So, have you finished your history report yet?"

"Ugh—don't remind me." I gave him a little shove. "Let's go swimming."

"After I just turned over? And ruin my great tan?…Okay, you're on."

And we jumped up to splash in the water.

CHAPTER 3

I got home at around 5:30, and my mom was in her study, typing away at something.

She's always working on stories and poems and stuff. I guess you could say writing is the love of her life. She used to be a therapist, but then four years ago she realized she really wanted to "free her creative energy" and so she started writing. She'd already gotten pretty good at it: she'd had four short stories published and was working on her first novel, and she just quit her old job. I was glad, because she seemed a lot happier now.

I stood in the doorway, looking at the back of her short curly brown hair and feeling a lot of love for her.

"Hi mom. Can I come in a second?"

"Oh hi, dear. Come on in. When did you get back from the gorge?"

"Just a minute ago. It was good, and not too crowded either." I went in and stood next to her at her computer. I put my right arm around her pudgy shoulders. I used to be embarrassed she was a little fat, but now I don't worry about it. "How're the Bartners?" They're the main characters in her new novel.

"Okay. They're struggling. God, I'm not quite sure what to do with them today." She stared at the screen for a few seconds, then turned and kissed my cheek. "So you had a nice day?"

"Yeah, it was fun. We talked about the prom—we're all getting psyched about it." I leaned over and looked at what she was typing.

"Good, I'm glad…Do you know when you're going to shop for your dress?"

"Tomorrow after school maybe, or next weekend. Don't bug me about it."

"I'm not bugging you."

I rolled my eyes at her.

"I take it you don't want me to ask you about it anymore?" she said.

"Right."

"Okay, okay. Will you set the table by six?"

"Sure. See you later."

"Yup," she said. On my way upstairs, I could hear her keyboard click-clacking away again.

She was a pretty good mom. Sometimes she could be a pain or nosy, but most of the time she knew when to lay off. And when I had a problem and wanted to talk to her, which wasn't that often, she could be pretty helpful.

I wished I could tell her about being gay, though, and about liking Tina. I could have, but I was scared she'd tell everyone or, even worse, be disappointed or angry. I wasn't sure exactly what I was afraid of. She did have a gay male friend from college, so she'd probably be understanding; both my parents were kind of liberal in fact. But I still felt too scared to tell them.

I lay on my bed and thought about the prom. It would probably be fun: I loved dancing, and it'd be fun to be with everyone. Even if Tina didn't go, it'd still be great.

I've always loved to dance. I love just moving around to Top 40 music and not worrying about how I look—it's a blast! At least being gay, I don't get self-conscious around guys. Freida and I once practiced here and she's pretty good, but when she's around guys I can see how she just tenses up. I bet I'd be that tense if I was dancing with Tina. Or some other cute girl. (Tina's NOT the only girl in the world, I reminded myself.) Sometimes it's not even whether they're cute or not but whether I thought there was even a slight chance they could be lesbian and could be interested.

Once when I was twelve, I thought a girl named Mary at sleep-away camp liked me, and I'm almost positive she was gay. I'd catch her staring at me or other girls and then she'd blush and look away. And she didn't seem interested in guys or teen romance books, either. In a group, she'd be really friendly to me, and we'd even roll our eyes and smirk to ourselves a little when everyone else was discussing boyfriends and crushes. But whenever we ended up alone together in the cabin or outside, Mary would make up an excuse to get away. I guess she was scared. God, I was, too. But she seemed more frightened than even I was. Oh well, I just hoped someday, something would work out with someone.

My thoughts were interrupted by my sister Becky's knock at the door.

"Yo, Sarah, mom says to set the table; it's almost dinner time."

"Yeah, I'm coming."

Becky is 14. She's okay. We're really different: she's into makeup, fancy hair-styles, designer clothing, and giggling with her friends on the phone. Occasionally I feel close to her if we get into a good conversation, but usually we just kid around superficially and argue and stuff.

I went down to set the table in a good mood. Maybe I'd go out bird-watching after supper. Bird listening, actually. I usually just walked around the neighborhood, especially where there were a lot of trees and bird feeders, and listened to their chirping. I loved doing that, and I had hardly any homework tonight. Studying for finals could wait another week, too.

I wondered if Dad was home yet. Dad's cool and is a pretty nice guy. He's always talking with the elderly women on our street and really listens to their problems. And he's into environmental stuff, often going down to the recycling drop-off center to help out or organizing clean-ups at the park. I probably got into bird-watching through his love of the outdoors. But he doesn't pressure me to do what he does; that's what I love about him. And I like that he can really listen when I confide in him once in a while.

Dad came into the dining room at 6:00 with a casserole he'd heated up.

"Oh hi, dad, you're home."

"Yup. I needed to get out of the office." He's a research biologist and sometimes jokes about what a pain the job is, but when serious, he says he enjoys most aspects of the work, which is great.

"Hmm. I thought it was mom's turn to cook."

"It was, but I switched with her since she was so caught up in her current chapter. How was your day?" His curly brown hair was sticking out a bit, I noticed. That and his slightly sagging stomach and shirt hanging down made him look sad or something. I did love him, though, and I liked how he really always wanted to know about what was happening in my life.

"Okay. I went swimming with Jarod after school." I set the plates and silverware out quickly and plopped down.

"It sounds like your day was relaxing," he said after a minute, as Becky and mom joined us. "So is he your boyfriend?" he teased, as mom and Becky came in.

"No, dad," I laughed pretending to throw a roll at him. "You've asked me a million times—he's just my friend!"

"Well, you know I'd love to have him as a son-in-law. But I'm sure you'll find a nice boy soon."

"Right, dad." I'd had enough of this topic.

We all served ourselves, so I thought I'd escaped the dreaded subject. Mom told us all about her latest chapter, and dad told us more about the research study he was working on.

Then Becky said, "Guess what? Can I tell you all about Bruce?" She ran her hand excitedly through her short curly light brown hair, similar to dad's but styled in a soft way about her face.

"Sure, dear. Who's Bruce?" said mom, serving herself more casserole. I practically choked on my milk.

"He's great." Becky was almost singing the words. "I met him at Cathy's party. He's a junior. He's tall with big muscles, and he's on the wrestling team. And he has the most beautiful red hair and freckles. You must know him, Sarah. He's in your grade."

I scowled under my breath. Bruce and his friends, including his cousin Mindy who was in my homeroom, made tons of anti-gay jokes at school. I'd heard them once yell "Lezzies" at two girls who were hugging hello in the hallway, and I'd heard Bruce calling some people "faggots" or "queers" in a loud voice if he didn't like them. I never knew what to do at those times, but it just made me want to kill him. Definitely, I hoped Bruce and Becky didn't hit it off, start going steady, and hang out together a lot, especially not here. I also knew there wasn't anything I could do about it. I hoped Becky could find a guy she liked, but then again, I didn't want any boyfriend of hers being a pain for me.

"Oh, yeah, yeah. I do know him."

"How well do you know him?"

"Not real well. He's okay."

"Just okay? He's great. Dad, you'd like him, he loves being outdoors."

(Yeah, I thought, to hunt animals and harass women.)

"You'd love him, too, mom," Becky continued. "Anyway, I'm seeing him Friday night. He'll pick me up here, so you two can get to meet him."

God, have him cancel, I prayed.

"Well, dear," said mom, "He sounds nice. I'll look forward to being introduced."

I groaned inwardly and tried to change the subject again, away from Bruce. "Well, even though I don't have a special someone," I commented, keeping the pronouns neutral, "I'm still psyched about the dance."

"Good for you, Sarah. One definitely does not need a boyfriend to live a happy or fulfilled life," said my mother thoughtfully. "When I met your father, part of me resisted getting involved for a long time. I just wanted to be free to work on my career and have fun. It took me several months to realize I truly *did* want a boyfriend and eventually a husband and kids."

"That's right," my dad kissed the top of her head as he got up to get some more water. "I brought her to her senses; I just swept her right off her feet."

"Dad, you did not! You said you were scared, too," laughed Becky.

"Okay, okay, so I was chicken for a while. But anyway, I'm glad you two are both taking it slow with dating."

Becky and I looked at each other. "Not always by choice," Becky said, and we laughed.

"Your time will come," dad said, smiling, "just make sure we get grandchildren, okay?," and he raised his eyebrows, opened his eyes wide, and blinked in an exaggerated way.

Becky and I rolled our eyes and groaned.

"Bye, dad," said Becky, gathering up her stuff.

"Yeah, see you later dad," I added, taking my plate to the dishwasher.

"What did I say?" dad joked with mom, as I headed upstairs.

Dad loves to pretend to pressure us. Still, I knew there was some truth to his jokes about grandchildren and it added to my fears of coming out to him and mom. I wasn't sure if I wanted kids and even whether a lover and I would be allowed to adopt or be inseminated.

Of course, then my mind drifted to a vivid image of Tina and I…and our children…

Then I stopped. "Enough!" I said out loud to my bedroom. All I needed to do tonight was my homework and figure out when to go buy my dress. Potential girlfriend or no potential girlfriend, I was determined to have a great time at the dance.

CHAPTER 4

"Hey, Sarah," called Freida. "What about this one over here?" She held up a dark blue dress. There must have been a hundred different styles at the "Dress Your Best" store. I didn't know where to start; at least Freida is a suave shopper. I'm glad she offered to come with me.

"Yeah, maybe. How much?" My mom said I could spend $150 since I could wear it for formal events at college, too.

"$129."

"That's pretty good. Let me try on a couple of sizes."

As I headed towards the dressing room, I ran smack into Tina. My heart jumped.

"Hi Sarah!" She seemed genuinely glad to see me, and maybe even a little nervous. "What are you doing here?"

"Shopping for a dress for the dance. How about you?" Breathe, I told myself when I noticed my heart pounding wildly.

"The same. Plus some more jeans without holes: mother's orders, you know."

I nodded my head. "Yeah, mine made me throw out a pair last week."

Then Freida came up behind us. "Hey, girl!" She and Tina gave each other the high five. "What's happening?"

"Shopping, of course. Comparing notes on the latest fashions with Sarah."

"So," Freida said, getting right to the question I'd been dying to ask, "Are you coming with all of us to the dance?"

"Yeah, yeah, I'm glad that you mentioned it. I've been thinking it would be fun to go with the bunch of you and not the people I used to hang out with."

She looked at the ground and shuffled her feet a bit. "So, yeah, that will be good."

She and I smiled nervously at each other. Meanwhile, the conversation in my head started going back and forth: "She is gay and she likes me" and "Stop imagining things. You're crazy, there's no way." I tried to ignore my head and listen to their conversation.

Freida and Tina discussed the times to meet, and then Tina split and Freida and I went into the dressing room. I tried to act calm so that Freida wouldn't notice anything.

I cleared my throat. "Well, that's great. I'm glad she'll be going with us." I tried to sound casual as I hung up the dress and peeled off my sweater.

"Yeah. I like her. I think she'll get along well with our gang," she pondered. "So how do you like these dresses?"

"I'm not sure yet; I'll let you know in a sec." I got busy trying the first one on. Meanwhile, my heart was pounding. Tina would be coming with us to the dance!

"You know," said Freida, leaning against the wall of the dressing room, "I kind of wish I had a date for the dance, even though I'm psyched to be going with our whole group."

"Which guy do you have in mind now?" I couldn't help asking, as I checked out the blue dress in the mirror. I wanted to know, but then I knew she'd probably ask me who I liked, and I hated having to deal with that.

"Aaron. I can't seem to get over that dumb crush. I wish I could get him out of my head…Well, that dress looks nice."

"Thanks. I want to see if they have my size in purple." I took it off and tried on the next one.

"So how about you?," Freida asked.

"What?"

"You know. Are you interested in anyone?"

Not that question again, I thought to myself. I hoped she couldn't read my mind. I really wished I could tell her the truth, but I didn't know how cool she'd be with it. I'd heard her make a few comments over the last few years, like that a certain guy seemed "faggy" or that a girl looked "dykey" in a particular outfit, which bothered me of course. But I also sensed she was just kind of saying it without thinking, that deep down she'd probably be okay with someone who was open about being lesbian or gay. I didn't feel ready to risk telling her though. Somehow telling a straight female friend seemed scarier than telling Jarod. I think because other girls might be more threatened and think I was coming on to them, when in reality I'd only come on to another girl I thought was or could be gay and who I liked. Also, I'm not thrilled with the possibility of being gay-bashed. Freida was waiting for my answer, since I seemed to be hesitating.

"Well, uh, yeah…Yeah, I do have my eye on a special someone. Doesn't everyone?" I tried to make a light joke of it.

"Yeah, usually. So who is he?"

"Well, it's uh…" I coughed. Lying was not my forte. "It's, uh, Jarod. But like I said before, I think he just likes me as a friend. And you know I might just feel that way too. Maybe I'm not ready for love yet." There, I hoped that would satisfy her.

"You don't have to love a guy—just go out with him!"

"I know, I know." I tried to laugh. My throat felt tight. I didn't like this conversation at all.

"You and Jarod are pretty close, but yeah, it doesn't seem like you two would go out or fall in love or anything."

"Yeah, maybe we are better off as just friends…So are you interested in anyone at *all* besides Aaron?" I just wanted to get the focus off me. Even though I'd been somewhat honest about me and Jarod, I *hated* everything I was covering up.

"Well, I also like Tommy, Gus, José, and David." We both laughed. "I figured it'd keep my options open."

"They're certainly open all right…Well, I'm going to go get that first dress in purple." I ran and got a purple one in my size off the rack, while Freida guarded our stuff in the dressing room.

When I got back, her mind was still on the dance. "Actually, since nothing will probably ever happen with Aaron, I'm hopeful that something really might happen with Tommy. At least at the dance, I'll have a clearer idea of where I stand."

"Mmm. Yeah, I know what you mean." I thought of Tina.

"You do? But I thought you already know that you and Jarod aren't meant to be together."

"Uh, well, that's true, but I just know how you feel in general, I mean."

She laughed. "Oh, yeah. Well, I hope I find out once and for all with Aaron and Tommy. And if you do get interested in anyone, just don't go after my guys."

"Well, you've taken half the eleventh grade."

She hit me in the arm and laughed.

"But seriously," I said. "Don't worry. I won't take any of them. And hey, I think I'll get this dress. What do you think?"

"Great. It looks pretty snazzy."

"Thanks. I'll go pay for it. Then do you want to go to the CD store and pet store?"

"Okay."

I got dressed and we went to the cashier.

While on line, Freida poked me and said "Hey, look at those dykes over there."

I turned the way she was pointing. One had a short crewcut and a long hanging earring in her left ear, a stud in the other ear, and a necklace with two big women's symbols on it. The other also had a real short haircut with one long, thin braid in the back, and she was wearing a tee-shirt with a big pink triangle saying "Silence = Death" in the middle. They looked a little older than us, probably from one of the colleges nearby. They *definitely* looked like lesbians.

My face got red. I was torn between the curiosity of seeing the women and how they looked, confusion about how she would know they were lesbians, and anger at her homophobic comment.

I looked back at Freida and took a deep breath.

"Yeah, but so what? They're just people."

"I know. I just thought they looked interesting, that's all. You don't have to get so high and mighty."

"I'm not. I just felt uncomfortable with it. I don't like the word 'dyke.' I...I heard someone who was gay once say she doesn't like when other people call her that." I played it cool, though my heart was pounding.

She looked at me a second, then said, "Yeah, you're right. It can be a real put-down. Sorry."

"No big deal. Let's just forget it." For the second time that day, I had to tell myself to keep breathing.

We went to the counter and I paid for my dress, and the conversation turned to our favorite music group.

As we headed for the record store, I still hadn't stopped sweating. That confrontation had felt really uncomfortable. Still, I was glad I had said something, because those anti-gay comments really piss me off! I almost just couldn't keep my anger in any longer! Maybe with someone like Bruce or Mindy, I wouldn't bother, because I know they're such hopeless cases. But if someone was my friend, I was beginning to feel like I had to say something.

Part of me wanted her and everyone else to know about me, and part of me still hoped people wouldn't get suspicious of me at the dance or anytime. And that people wouldn't make homophobic jokes towards anyone. I didn't want any more confrontations.

CHAPTER 5

"Mom! He'll be here in five minutes and I'm nowhere near ready!"

Becky was frantic. She ran into the bathroom with her makeup case. Dad and I looked at each other while watching T.V. in the den.

"Women!," he joked. "Can't live with them, can't live without them."

"I can live without her. I just hope I'm not like that for the dance tomorrow."

"Well, if not tomorrow, in time. You're young, just wait till you're in love."

God, if he only knew I was gay: what would what he think?

I could hear the doorbell ring a few minutes later. I was glad I was safe in the den, away from Bruce. I heard my mom answer the door and chat with him, then Becky coming downstairs and the three of them talking.

Then mom called out, "Honey? And Sarah? Come and say hello to Bruce."

Oh no, I thought to myself. I was afraid this was going to happen.

"Dad, do we have to?" I looked at dad, knowing full well what he would say.

"Well, I'd like to meet him. And two minutes of friendliness won't kill you."

I decided I might as well be nice, for Becky's sake.

We went out to the living room, and dad shook hands with Bruce.

"Hi, how's it going?" I greeted him politely.

"Hi, Sarah."

Then mom said, "Well, have fun, I'll let you teenagers all talk. Nice meeting you Bruce."

"Me too, nice meeting you, Bruce," dad said.

"Yeah, nice meeting you, Mr. and Mrs. Goldberg."

Right after my parents walked off, I was about to say my goodbyes when Becky said, "Oh, I forgot something. I'll be right back," and she ran upstairs. I moaned inwardly.

Bruce and I looked at each other.

"Your family seems nice," he said.

"Yeah, they are." And I added silently: be nice to my sister. I sat down on the sofa resignedly.

"So are you going to the dance tomorrow?," he asked, flipping through a magazine on the coffee table.

"Yeah, it should be fun. You?"

"Yeah. I wouldn't miss it. Who are you going with?"

"Oh, a bunch of my friends: Freida, Jarod, and that whole group."

"No boyfriend yet?"

"Nope." God, what is this, the third degree?

"Better get one soon or the guys will give you up for gay!"

I would've loved to have punched him. "Maybe," I said carefully, not wanting to seem defensive or angry, though of course I was.

He gave me a quizzical look.

"Who are you going with?," I said quickly, to change the subject.

"Oh, probably the guys. And meet up with Mindy, Brenda, and that crowd. Maybe even Becky would come with me if we hit it off tonight. You wouldn't mind, would you?"

"No, of course not," I lied, as if my opinion would matter to him anyway.

Just then, Becky came bounding back down the stairs. "Sorry to keep you waiting, Bruce." I had to admit to myself she looked beautiful.

"That's okay. Well, nice chatting with you, Sarah. Should we head out?" he asked her, all manners.

"Yeah, let's go. Bye Sarah," she said, and they left.

I walked back to the den.

"Well, he seems nice," my mom said to me, smiling. "And now, I'm going to go hibernate in my study and write a little."

Dad and I looked at each other after she left the room.

"I'm glad you went out there and were friendly," dad said.

"Thanks. I really don't like him that much."

"You don't? How come?" He played with the remote control for the T.V.

"Ah…It's a long story. Maybe I'll tell you in ten years."

He looked like he wanted to ask me more, but then decided against it. "Okay. But like him or not, you kids are still young enough that we do wait up.

So don't be surprised to find me and your mother up late tonight—and tomorrow."

"Fine. As long as you're waiting up for Becky and me equally."

"Yup. You know we love you, right?"

"Yeah. Parents!"

"Kids!," he joked back.

I settled down to watching T.V., forgetting about Bruce and trying to just enjoy the show.

CHAPTER 6

Now it was my turn to be dressing up, going out, and to be nervous. The limousine was all arranged: Jarod would be picked up first, then me, then Freida, Wendell, Gus, Abdul, Sylvia, Tommy, Libby, and Tina last.

Tina! My heart skipped a beat. I was so glad she'd be coming with us. And even though I knew she was probably straight, I knew that if she was gay she wouldn't necessarily be interested in me. Still, I couldn't help hoping. She was a nice person, and I would at least like to get to know her as a friend. Then I told myself that I'd had enough fantasy indulgence for the night. I just had to go to the dance, have fun, try to get to know Tina, talk to everyone, and dance, dance, dance.

After I put on my purple dress and was all ready, I went downstairs to wait. My parents looked up from the books they were reading.

"Hey, you look great, Sarah." My dad seemed proud.

"My, you certainly do look beautiful." My mom smiled, too.

Becky came walking through from the kitchen. "I wanted to see for myself. You do look nice!"

"Thanks." I wasn't used to all the attention, and so I started to blush.

I think dad could tell, because he said, "Okay, let's leave her be." Then he winked at me and went back to his book.

"Well," Becky said, playing with her bangs, "if you see Bruce, tell him to go jump in a lake."

I looked at her in surprise. "Why? What happened last night? I didn't even think to ask you today."

"It wasn't great. He's a jerk, I'll just say that. And horny as hell." She whispered this last part in my ear.

"Did he try to force you to do anything?," I whispered back.

"No, he was just hoping."

I laughed. "Well, somehow it doesn't surprise me that you didn't like him."

"Well, he sure caught me off guard." She seemed sad.

"That must have been a drag. You were probably hoping to have a great time."

"I know it."

"Well, you deserve better. There are plenty of nice guys out there."

"Yeah, you're right. Thanks, Sarah." She gave me a big hug.

I was so relieved she didn't like him. At least now I didn't have to worry about him hanging out here all the time.

I went by the front window to watch for the limo. The only time I'd ever ridden in one before was for a relative's funeral, which was pretty depressing. Tonight would be a lot different.

The phone rang then. I picked up, and an elderly voice on the other end said, "Hello darling! How's my prom girl?"

"Grandma! Hi!" My heart jumped. "But it's not the prom till next year. It's just the junior dance." I wished I'd called her recently—it had been a whole month! And I hadn't gone down to see her at the nursing home in Binghamton since March.

"Still, it's an important event. How are you?"

"Great, grandma. Did you call just to talk to me?" I was grinning from ear to ear. If anyone could help me feel good, it was grandma, my mother's mom.

"Yes. I had it on my calendar to call you tonight."

"Oh, well I'm glad. The limo will be here any minute."

"Wonderful. I still can't believe you're going in such a fancy car, with a hired driver no less."

"I know. It is funny." I plopped down on a soft chair and giggled. "Maybe you could ride in one someday."

"Only when I'm in my coffin."

"Grandma! Don't talk like that."

"Okay, okay, I'm sorry. So are you all set?"

"Yeah, but I'm nervous. You know, all the pressure to be going out with someone, and nervousness about whether someone I like might like me."

"I understand. It was exactly the same for me at your age. So who is this guy you like?"

"Oh, no one worth mentioning." Shit, the same old hiding who I am, I thought. "Maybe I'll tell you one day if anything happens between us."

"That would be wonderful, Sarah dear. And I hope you just have a wonderful time tonight. Remember I love you."

"Thanks, grandma."

The door bell rang then.

"Oh, there's the limo. I love you, too, and thanks so much for calling me."

"My pleasure. Bye darling."

"Bye."

My heart felt full from her having called. Even though I wasn't out to her about being a lesbian, I always just felt so good when I talked to her or saw her. With grandma, I didn't obsess about anything. I felt free for a little while. I just felt totally loved.

I took a deep breath and then ran and looked through the window. Sure enough, I could see there was a big, white limousine outside.

"Have a wonderful time," said mom, who had come out to see me leave.

And dad said, "Have fun. Sweep those boys off their feet"

I didn't think I'd be doing any sweeping of boys, but I yelled, "Thanks! See you later," and I opened the door.

"Sarah Goldberg, I presume? Danny's Executive Limousine, at your service." The chauffeur had on a fancy white uniform and everything.

"Great! Bye everyone." I waved good-bye to my parents one last time and followed him down the driveway.

CHAPTER 7

❀

I climbed into the limousine and gave Jarod a hug.

"Hey," he smiled. "You're looking snazzy."

"Thanks. You look pretty good yourself." He had on a dark blue suit with a flashy blue and purple tie that were really becoming. He wore his shirt button open part way down and his tie real loose, like the laid-back friend I knew and loved. His hair was tied back neatly, too.

He pointed out to me that the band tying it back was pink, a "subtle hint for Gus, in case he happens to stare into my hair."

"Yeah, right," I teased. It was almost impossible to see the pink unless someone pointed it out. But I knew how he felt; after all, I was wearing purple underwear, and no one would be seeing that tonight.

"So, beautiful, I'm excited that everyone's coming."

"Yeah, handsome. So Freida's getting picked up next, right?" I asked.

"Right, and Tina's coming, did you hear?"

I blushed. "Yeah." I looked at him. "And your two crushes will be with us tonight, too, I haven't forgotten that," I teased him.

"Yup. We'll see. I just want to have fun tonight."

"Me too."

We were quiet for a few minutes. It felt nice to be able to be honest, at least with Jarod, about who I was interested in.

One by one everyone got picked up by the limo. It was great to see everyone all dressed up. The guys all had on suits, though Gus had on a black and pink polka dotted tie and buttons with jokes on them like "Born to Party" and "I have two left feet but don't tell anyone." ("I'm rebelling against the formality of it all. It makes me nervous!," he said). The girls all had on dresses. Tina looked fantastic in her dark pink dress and long earrings. My heart was definitely fluttering, but I just said how nice she looked, the same as I said to everyone else.

We all seemed ready for a really good time. I wondered if the others felt as nervous as I did about people they had crushes on. Sylvia and Wendell seemed to be flirting, and Jarod was just talking casually with his crushes Gus and Libby. Mostly, though, everyone just seemed relaxed and talking with everyone. As we pulled into the parking lot, we all joked about who would make up the weirdest dances.

We headed toward the gym, and already we could hear the music blasting. A couple of other limousines were there too, though most kids seemed to have walked or had gotten dropped off by parents. A limo definitely felt classy.

"Did you go to the sophomore dance last year?" I asked Tina, as we walked next to each other. I couldn't tell if my heart was beating because I was excited hearing the music or because I was excited to be talking to her, or both.

"No, I wasn't into it last year."

"Really, how come?" I looked at her curiously.

"I guess it just didn't feel like my scene." She looked at the ground. "Now I just figure even if it's not exactly my thing to go to one of these dances, it's nice to go anyway and just hang out with people."

I wondered if it wasn't her scene because she might be gay.

She looked up. "How about you?"

"Oh, I've always liked dancing, but it's easier doing it in my living room than here. Last year I came but just with Freida and Sylvia, and we mostly stood around. I think it'll be more fun tonight with this big group."

"Yeah." She smiled at me. "I hope those teachers aren't watching us like hawks or anything."

"I know," I said, smiling back at her. "I can just see Mr. Vantam like a vulture, swooping down if a couple gets too close." I acted out an imitation of a huge bird descending upon its prey, and she cracked up laughing.

Some of the others joined us and we acted out some of the other teachers while we waited in line to hand in our tickets. I began to feel a lot more comfortable; I think we all did.

The music sounded great. Most people were dressed up, though there were a few other rebels like Gus. The gym was decorated with red and golden streamers, green balloons, and two of those disco balls on the ceiling which reflect moving light speckles everywhere. They were pretty.

At first we all danced in a group. Sylvia and Wendell were the winning clowns of the evening, making up weird steps which we'd all copy. Then we all broke into smaller groups or pairs, chatted and then switched. It all had a nice flow to it. And we danced some with other people we hadn't come with.

One guy, John, who I knew from math class, seemed to be flirting with me. He was smiling a lot and kept seeming to end up dancing next to me for a while. I felt uncomfortable, and so I started moving away and looking at other people more. He seemed to get the hint after a while and he went back to his other friends. God, I thought, if he only knew just how totally he had been wasting his time!

It was fun chatting with Tina between songs and while dancing sometimes. We talked about our classes and our parents a bit. She told me how she and her old friends had grown apart over the last year.

About Bruce's cousin, Tina said, "Mindy and I just don't get along anymore. We just have different values about things". But she didn't explain exactly what she meant, and then she switched the topic to music groups.

I knew that, like Bruce, Mindy was homophobic and just prejudiced in general. I wondered if that was why they weren't friends anymore.

We were chatting some more about music and our favorite singers several minutes later when Mindy, Bruce, and another girl Helen walked by. I could feel my hands automatically clench up a bit.

"Hey, what's happening?" Mindy and Bruce both said. Mindy gave Tina a weird look, like tense or angry or something. I could tell that she and Tina were keeping their distance.

"Not much," said Tina. I glanced at her. Her face muscles looked tensed up, too.

I just kind of smiled politely at them, hoping they'd go away.

Bruce looked at me. "So, did Becky tell you about her date with me?"

"No, not much."

"Yeah, well she got really mad at me. That girl has no sense of humor! She acted like I was a pig for just wanting to kiss her."

I knew it was more than that but I didn't say so. "Hmm. Well, maybe you're not meant for each other."

"Yeah. I guess not."

"So no hot guys for you two tonight?" Mindy said, a bit sarcastically. I wondered why she was asking.

Tina and I glanced at each other, both of us, I was sure, wishing they'd just go away.

"No," said Tina casually. "Sarah and I are just watching for now."

"Well, you two should go dance with some cute guys. You wouldn't want anyone to think you two are dykes, would you?"

I wanted to punch her. And I could sense Tina was angry, too.

"Come off it, Mindy," said Tina, looking her in the eye. "Let's just drop it."

"Excuuuuuse me," said Mindy. "I'm sorry if it hit a little too close to home."

"Why don't you just leave us alone?!" said Tina.

"Calm down," tossed back Mindy. "What's your problem? Are you scared everyone will know?"

"No!," said Tina loudly. "I just wish you'd get off my case!"

For a second I imagined Mindy as an inflatable doll that I practiced punching on as a kid.

Freida came by and stood behind us, listening.

Mindy said, "I'm not on your case, neither of you two dykes."

And Bruce and Helen just stood behind her, watching our reactions and smirking at us.

Tina clenched her fists and stepped towards Mindy, and Mindy took a step towards her.

I was frozen. I was torn between wanting to hold Tina back so she wouldn't get hurt and wanting to step forward with her and clobber Bruce while we were at it.

Before I knew what had happened, Freida stepped right in between them.

"Hey, Tina, everyone wants to dance with you and Sarah," she said. "Let's not waste our time with idle chatter." She gently pushed Tina back towards our group. When Freida saw Tina take a small step backwards, she added "Come on. It's not worth it, let's go." She could be very commanding when she needed to be.

Freida gently pushed us back towards our group.

Tina tossed one last look over her shoulder and coolly walked back towards our group.

Mindy called out, "Yeah, see you homos," in a menacing tone.

We ignored her as we walked back towards our friends. My heart was pounding. I was so glad Freida had stepped in. I'm sure we could've really gotten into a fight and then ended up suspended or something worse.

"Geez," said Freida. "They can be such jerks! What started them up?"

After a pause, Tina said "Mindy has just acted like a jerk since we've stopped hanging out."

"Yeah, things can be tense with someone after you've stopped being friends. I've been through that kind of stuff too," said Freida.

"That's especially hard if they're making derogatory comments all the time, too" I said.

"Yeah, I really can't stand to be around her anymore." Tina's face was still tense and bright red.

Neither Freida nor I asked her outright about being called gay or if she was a lesbian, but God was I blown away! It seemed more likely now that maybe Tina really was gay, and that certainly made me happy. Freida seemed to be suspecting Tina was gay, too, and still seemed comfortable with Tina. If that were true, maybe my friends would even accept me being gay if I decided to tell them. It was a lot to think about.

"Well," said Freida. "I promised Tommy another dance tonight. Does my hair look okay?"

"You look wonderful," I said. And she did: her long blond curls shone in the neon lights.

She smiled and walked away to go find him. I felt grateful she'd been there.

The dance was relatively uneventful after that. Mindy, Bruce, and crowd stayed away, and it was really fun hanging out with Tina, Jarod, Freida, and everyone else. Freida and Tommy seemed to be getting together, along with Sylvia and Wendell. And at the very least, me and Tina were getting to know each other. It definitely felt really good to be among friends, no matter what the future would hold.

CHAPTER 8

❁

Things went on much as normal for the rest of June, as much as they can with classes ending and finals starting up. Freida treated me the same as usual, while Mindy and I ignored each other if we passed in the hallways. Jarod and I still swam at the gorge two or three times a week and discussed life, friends, school, and, of course, our crushes.

It felt different now to talk to Tina. I knew almost for sure that she was gay, and though I hadn't gotten up my nerve to discuss it, I figured she guessed I was, too. And we were really becoming friends.

Tina and I called each other a few times a week to shoot the breeze, and we got together once to play basketball. She even said she was interested in going bird-watching with me sometime, so we planned to do that soon after our last final. And now talking with Jarod about it and thinking about it on my own, I didn't feel as nervous or heart-fluttery. I just felt calm and patient with the friendship and accepting whatever would happen.

Today Jarod and I decided to meet for an hour's study break and swim.

"So have you heard about that summer job yet?" he asked, getting himself cozy on a rock.

"Yeah. It looks pretty much all set. I just have to go fill out my forms and stuff." I was going to be working at a biology lab at the university, working for someone my father knew. "I'm pretty psyched about it—it sure beats working at the clothing warehouse like last summer."

"Yeah, you really were miserable there."

"How about you?" I said. "You must be pretty excited yourself!"

Jarod was going to a college in Quebec for the summer, on a "Learn French Quick" program for high school students. He loved everything French.

"Yeah," he said, "I can't wait. I can't believe I"m really going."

"Well, I'll miss you. It won't be the same around here without you. But I know that program will be fantastic!"

"Thanks. I'll miss you, too. I'll send you…well, at least one letter."

"You better."

"And you better write me, too. I want to know about everything: your family, job, love life, the birds, all of it!"

"You know I'll definitely tell you everything, especially about Tina. You're the only one I talk to about her."

"Really?" Jarod turned and looked at me. "I'd forgotten that."

"Yeah. I'm too afraid to even talk to Tina about being gay."

"Wow. I wish you had other gay or bisexual people to talk to."

"Me too. I could call the gay hotline at the college, but I've been too chicken."

He was quiet for a few seconds. "I guess you have to be ready. And you and Tina haven't even come out to each other yet."

"Yeah. I think I'm afraid to really say it and acknowledge to another lesbian that it's true."

"It will pop out when you're ready."

"I hope so." Then I thought aloud, "I wonder if I could even meet a lot of other gay people our age somehow so we could all hang out and do things and go places. Hmm." It felt neat to think about it.

"Sounds good," said Jarod.

I thought about how there must be other gay kids at school or at the other high school: there was supposed to be 10%, right? Maybe I could start a group. But how to find them if I didn't even know if they really existed?

Jarod and I hung out for a while longer and then we each headed home to study. I knew I really needed to tell Tina I was gay. If I couldn't tell her, another lesbian (or probable lesbian), who could I tell? And how would I ever tell my parents?

I was determined to tell Tina, and I was determined to tell her *soon*.

CHAPTER 9

Tina and I had been on the trail for over an hour. I was glad we'd made these plans to made plans to hike and birdwatch together, two of my favorite activities.

"What's that one?" she asked. We stopped and watched and listened for a while: its song sounded really beautiful.

"Oh, that's a black-capped chickadee." I loved it when people were really interested in birds and asked me about them. We watched and listened to it a while longer, then walked on.

We chatted on and off as we walked along the trail. Tina told me about the artwork she did, mostly charcoal sketching and watercolor. She hoped to go to a school with a good art department for college.

We started getting pretty hungry around noon and looked for a place to sit and eat the lunches we had each packed.

We found a log in a little clearing and sat down.

"Ah, this drink of water feels so good after those three miles," she remarked.

"Yeah, I'm starved, too."

We ate our tuna sandwiches for a while in silence. It seemed like a miracle to feel so comfortable around her after all those times my crush had made me so nervous to even talk with her. It felt good to be real friends, whatever else might or might not happen.

After a while, Tina said, "I'm so glad finals are over. Now I can finally relax and enjoy the summer."

"Definitely. I'm looking forward to my job, too. So did you hear back from any of those places you applied to?"

"Oh, yeah, didn't I tell you? I got the one teaching arts and crafts to kids at that summer arts day camp in July and August."

"Hey, great! You really wanted that, too."

"Yeah, I'm psyched. It will be neat. And it turns out the day camp is run by a gay man, too."

We looked at each other, then both looked away. Neither one of us had ever said the "G word" before, nor the "L word." We were quiet for a while.

After a minute, she said, "You too, right?"

"Yes," I said, swallowing hard. "You?"

"Yeah." She grinned. "God, I knew you must have figured it out about me, it was so obvious from what happened at the dance."

"Well, I'm sure everyone thought so, myself included, but I didn't want to 100% assume. It felt too good to be true in a way, to find another lesbian among my friends, or my new friends, anyway." I smiled too.

"Well, I'm glad we finally admitted it out loud. Now we can talk about it!"

"I know. I've never talked to another lesbian about it before, especially not one my own age. Did you?"

"Well, actually I had a girlfriend once."

I turned and looked at her again, stunned, impressed, jealous. "You did?? Who was she? How did it happen? I mean, that is, if you feel comfortable saying."

"Hmm…Well, she's pretty closeted. I promised her I wouldn't tell anyone. But I don't mind telling you <u>how</u> it happened."

"Okay." I giggled nervously. "So how did it happen?"

"Well…," Tina paused for dramatic effect, making faces. Then she chewed on her apple some.

"Come on! Tell me already!"

"Okay, okay. I just started hanging out a lot with a girl from school around two years ago. She was in my gym class the beginning of sophomore year. We just hit it off and got along real well. And even back then, some kids would call me a dyke or homo and make me the butt of jokes. I guess they just sensed it in me. Once in junior high, some kids locked me in a cabinet at the back of the classroom and the teacher needed a crowbar to get me out. It was pretty humiliating.

"Anyway, I did have some friends, including this girl from gym class. Well, a few months after we started hanging out outside of school, we were watching a VCR movie one day and she asked me if I wanted a backrub. I was surprised but said sure. I wasn't sure how she meant it, but I was attracted to her, so I figured I'd find out. So after I let her rub my back, she began kissing the back of my neck all of a sudden. So I turned around and kissed her on the lips, and the rest started from there. She said she hadn't been sure she was gay before, but that now she was. We were lovers for several months, about six, and then she got cold feet when her friends and family said we were spending too much time alone. So she ended the relationship, saying she couldn't handle it. And now, she acts totally straight and says she is, too."

"Wow! No kidding!"

"And you know what else? You know how Mindy acts so homophobic? I always thought that she might be attracted to girls, too. It's just a feeling, maybe from the way she watched some other girls. And she knew about the girl I was involved with, and I think she just couldn't handle that maybe she liked girls, too!"

"That would make sense then, that she acts like such a jerk towards you now."

"That's for sure." Tina rolled her eyes.

"Do your parents know?"

"No!" she said loudly, her face getting red. "I think my mom suspects but isn't sure, but I don't want to tell them. They're pretty conservative in a lot of ways. So I think they wouldn't really want to know, which is fine with me." She sounded a bit sad, though. We were both quiet for a minute.

"So how about you?" She raised her eyebrows at me. "What's your story? Any hot lovers in your past?"

"No, no lovers. Nothing's worked out yet. Once there was a girl at camp, but she was totally scared to talk to me when we were alone, let alone do anything. But when we were in groups, she certainly was sending me lots of eye contact and always touching me on the arm. It nearly drove me nuts!"

"I'll bet," Tina said. "Have you always known you were gay?"

"I've known since I was eight. At first, I didn't understand what it meant to be attracted to other girls, what it was called, what other people would think. But I knew it wasn't something you were supposed to talk about. After a while, since no one knew about me, I guess I just relaxed about it and accepted it more. And I read about homosexuality being okay in one of those advice columns, and that helped a lot. I don't know what I would have done without those." I noticed she was sitting a little closer to me. My face got hot and I felt warm energy running up and down my body.

"Yeah, those columns helped me, too. I felt like there was no one else for so long, and that I was totally screwed up. Now I know: I'm just gay, that's all, and that it's something to feel good about." She paused, then asked, "And your parents?"

"Well, I've never told them and I don't think they suspect. They're pretty liberal in general, so I think they might be okay with me being a lesbian. I really do want to tell them. But I'm petrified. I guess I'm just not ready yet."

"Yeah, it's a hard thing to do, but if you want to do it, you've got plenty of time."

"True."

My face still felt hot with her sitting so close to me. I stood up and brushed the crumbs off my lap. "So shall we keep hiking?"

"Sure," she said, looking into my eyes, then gathering up her stuff.

We mostly talked about less intense topics for the rest of the afternoon, though we did chat about who else at school might have gay potential. It was fun. I wondered to myself if maybe Tina had wanted to make a move on me back at lunch, but I also knew that she might not have. Maybe she hadn't realized how close we were sitting until we were. But I was definitely still shaky, and I was just glad to have the hike to focus on.

On the way home, we agreed to try another trail next weekend. Part of me couldn't wait, and the other part of me was petrified of being alone with her again.

Aargh!, I thought to myself, and I wished Jarod was still in Ithaca to talk to.

CHAPTER 10

I was excited to see my grandmother after so many months. I snuggled down in the slightly lumpy seat in the Greyhound bus, relaxing for the hour ride.

Of course, this gave me time to wonder what, if anything, would happen between me and Tina. I knew if I thought too much about it, it would make me nuts, so I tried to just sleep and think about seeing grandma.

I took a taxi from the Binghamton bus station to her nursing home. It was an old converted mansion, with three floors and an extension to the house built in back. There was a big back yard and side yard with beautiful gardens and flowers. It really was nice compared to other nursing homes I'd heard about. Most of the people who lived there, like grandma, could walk around a lot and had their heads still together; they just couldn't make their own meals or take care of their own place anymore.

Grandma was in her room reading a "large print" version of *Little Women* when I came in.

"Sarah! You're prettier than I expected. Let me give you a hug and kiss."

"It's great to see you, Grandma," I said as I hugged her. She smelled nice, too, like roses. She always wore the greatest perfumes.

"I'm glad to hear it. Now sit down and rest."

"Oh, grandma, I'm not tired, but I'll sit with you." I smiled lovingly and sat next to her on her small pink sofa. "What made you decide to read *Little Women*? It's for kids." I took it and looked fondly at the cover.

"I just saw it in the downstairs bookshelf today, and it reminded me of you: a little woman!"

"Thanks." I giggled. "I read that years ago, though."

"Well, you'll always be a little woman to me."

"I know." I breathed a deep breath. It was nice having a grandma. "Do you want to go walk and sit in the garden before lunch? It's sunny and warm out."

"That would be nice, dear." She put on her pale blue sweater, "just in case," and I watched her slowly button it up the front. Her pale wrinkled hands shook a little, and I couldn't help wondering if she looked thinner. I sighed and wrinkled my brow.

"Are you feeling okay, grandma?"

"Yes. Why do you ask?"

"No reason," I said. "It's just my prerogative as a granddaughter to worry a little."

"That's fair," she said, taking my arm. "But there's really nothing to worry about. Now, let's go to the garden, and you can tell me all about what's happening in your life."

We took the elevator down and walked slowly outside. I told her about the end of school, about my summer job, and about my various friends. I felt so comfortable, (I couldn't believe it) I even said, "I have my eye on someone special." I took a deep breath and looked at grandma and smiled.

"You *do*?" She gazed lovingly into my eyes and squeezed my hand. "That's wonderful dear. Who is he?"

She must have sensed my hand stiffen up, because she said, "It's okay, you don't have to tell me. No details. I just hope it works out, Sarah."

"Thanks. I hope it works out, too." I paused. "How about you, grandma?" I had never thought of grandma dating, but why not?

"Oh, I flirt with some of the men, but no one special. No one cute enough for me. I'll point my favorites out to you at lunch, though. Here, let's go play checkers."

We spent the rest of the day playing checkers, eating lunch, looking over her photograph albums, and just sitting together listening to the leaves stirring in the wind and a few sparrows calling to each other.

As always, it was so wonderful to just be with grandma, and when I hugged her goodbye, when the taxi pulled up in the late afternoon, I just felt so loved by her and so much love *for* her.

I said, "Hey grandma, I do sometime want to tell you about my someone special. I'm just…not ready."

"That's fine, Sarah. Whenever you're ready, you know I'm happy to listen. Now, give me a kiss and have a safe trip back."

I kissed her and then hugged her hard and ran for the cab. It felt so good to feel at peace with myself as I always did around grandma and, for once, to have a rest from all my obsessions and worrying. Everything would work out: with Tina, with grandma, with life. I hoped.

CHAPTER 11

The next Saturday was another sunny day, so Tina and I picked another trail and headed out.

We chatted about our summer jobs. My job at the biology lab was going pretty well, though I'd only been there a couple of days, and Tina would start at the summer arts camp on Tuesday.

"I can't wait to be around my gay boss, just to see what he's like," she said.

"Yeah, that's neat. Do you think he'll come out to you directly?"

"I don't know. But I'll probably try coming out there, so that might help."

"That's a good idea," I said, envious of her working in a gay environment.

My stomach muscles started doing acrobatics again from being alone with Tina. I wondered if anything would happen, if she'd make a move, if I would. I wanted to try holding her hand or saying something, but I was petrified. I also hoped she would do something, but I was terrified of that, too.

I tried to push everything out of my mind, but I still felt nervous through the whole morning of hiking. We finally stopped for lunch around 1:30.

Tina had brought us tuna sandwiches; I had the cola, chips, and fruit. We munched, chatted, and watched the blue jays and crows in the maple trees nearby. She threw them some bread, and several came closer to us to get it. The birds were gorgeous up close. I was finally able to relax and forget my nervousness, which was a relief. We sat for a while in silence, watching and listening to the birds and just enjoying the breeze and sunshine.

Then my heart just started beating fast again, as I thought about my friend sitting beside me, my friend who was also a lesbian, my friend who I had a crush on.

We looked at each other and we smiled, then looked away.

I didn't know what to do, so I decided to take a risk. I moved over and sat a little closer to her, like she had done last week.

Then she reached over and took my hand.

CHAPTER 12

꧁

I thought my heart would never stop beating. We just held hands and looked at each other, and then I leaned over and kissed her. She kissed me back.

"Wow," I said after a minute. I could hardly talk.

I took another deep breath. "I've never kissed anyone before," I admitted.

"Really?" she asked gently, looking at me with her wide blue eyes.

"Yeah. And it's nice with you. I'm glad you made the first move by holding my hand."

"Good." She giggled. "God, I was so nervous. I had a crush on you for so long, since we were in economics class together."

"Really?! Me, too," I said, hardly believing she liked me, let alone as long as I'd liked her. I'd spent so long trying *not* to get my hopes up, that it was hard now to let in the wonderful truth. "I wish we'd gotten to know each other sooner."

"Yeah, so do I. But at least we're getting to know each other now," she said, looking me in the eye and smiling.

I smiled back. "That's true." My stomach was still doing flip-flops inside of me.

She leaned over and we kissed again. Her lips felt responsive and soft, and then we kissed each other harder and put our arms around each other. I felt really turned on.

We kissed, hugged, and just sat close with our arms around each other for a while.

After a half hour or so, I felt scared and said, "Uh, let's take it slow. I feel nervous. It's all so new…"

"Yeah, of course. I'm totally scared, too."

"You are?" I thought only I was scared.

"Yeah, I am," and she playfully and gently wopped me on the head. Then we both cracked up laughing.

And then we just sat for a long while, with our arms around each other and holding hands. Then we slowly got up to begin the rest of our hike.

CHAPTER 13

I came into my house whistling, my heart still pumping intensely. I went upstairs to my bedroom, lay down, and thought about what had happened.

So I had a girlfriend, a real girlfriend—a lover! I couldn't believe it and I could believe it. I felt so happy and so scared. I'd finally met a girl who wasn't afraid to be gay, wasn't afraid to act on it, who I felt close to and could talk to, and who I felt attracted to and wanted to be with. Best of all, she felt the same way. I just wanted to sing and dance and smile forever.

I still had no idea what my straight friends would think, much less my parents. I guess I'd tell them all in time or they'd figure it out, whichever came first. I might not want to tell certain friends if they seemed too homophobic. I wasn't really sure what Freida would think; she'd stuck up for us at the dance, but then again she made those anti-gay comments sometimes. Actually, she hadn't made any since the dance, so I guessed she'd probably be okay with it. I didn't know for sure, though. I guessed that for all my friends, time would tell.

Despite all the horrible things I could imagine happening, I didn't regret being with Tina, and I was glad I was gay.

Tina and I had said we'd talk on the phone later that night, so I was looking forward to that.

There was someone else I wanted to talk to first, though. Thanking the heavens that there were long extension cords, I brought the phone into my room and dialed Jarod's number in Canada. I figured it would be worth the money for the call. I just prayed he'd be there.

I had to dial the main number of his summer program, then got transferred to his house phone, and finally his hallway phone.

He answered the phone, luckily, and I said "Jarod."

"Hey, Sarah! How are you?"

"Great. How are you?"

"Good. You're calling me all the way from Ithaca?"

"Yes," I laughed. "I just had to. Tina and I…um…talked and…"

"Talked?" he asked knowingly, teasingly. "And? What happened? Tell me!"

"I will!…Well, I think I'm in love."

"Wow! So when's the wedding? But no, seriously, that's great! How'd it happen?"

Briefly I told him the story. My heart started pounding again.

"Wow," he said again, after I'd told him the whole thing. "So how does it feel?"

"Scary, and good. I feel so happy and scared to death of what it means, I mean with being gay and the coming out and all. What if my parents disown me?"

"I don't think your particular parents will, but I know how scary that must be. When I had a crush on Louis a few years ago, I had nightmares of people stoning us to death and I'd get anxiety attacks, too."

"Really?" I couldn't talk for several seconds as I took this in. "I'm shocked. I had no idea—you seemed so blasé about being bisexual!"

"Yeah, well I think I kept a lot of my fears to myself. It took a while for me to get some perspective. You sound calmer than I was last year, but not being straight is scary, that's all there is to it."

"Yeah, I guess…I just wish you'd told me. I had no idea how hard it was for you! I could have supported you more."

Jarod paused and sighed. "Yeah, sorry…I should have told you."

We were quiet for a few seconds, and I took a deep breath.

Then I added, "Okay, thanks…I know, too, that it hasn't totally hit me yet, but a lot of people do hate lesbians and gays."

"That's for sure. Some people just get freaked out by gay people and want to hurt them."

"Yeah, that's what really scares me the most: how other people might react." I paused. "Well, I'm not going to broadcast my business to everyone. I just got involved today. I'm glad that Tina and I will have the summer to enjoy each other before we have to deal with everyone in school."

"But some people will figure it out, you know, friends or acquaintances you weren't going to tell, no matter how careful you are."

I felt excited and scared, both. "You think so?," I asked switching the phone to my other ear. "How?"

"Well, sometimes if you're in love with someone or even just have a crush on someone, it's hard to hide that moony-eyed look. Just think of Sylvia and Wendell or Freida and Abdul: they can never stop looking at each other."

"I guess you're right. And some people already suspect about Tina being a lesbian after that dance, maybe about me, too."

"Maybe you should try not to think about it for now. It's only been a couple of hours that you've been in a relationship."

"You're right, you're right." I laughed at myself.

"Well, congratulations. You're a really nice person and you deserve to have a girlfriend."

"Aw, shucks, Jarod." I felt happy he'd said that though.

"Okay, well, I've got to scoot. So I'll hear from you again soon?"

"Yeah, I'll definitely write, or I'll call again if I can afford it. And I'm still waiting for *your* first letter, sweety pie." I couldn't help needling him.

"Well, you know how I am with writing; but I still love getting your updates."

"Yeah, I know. Bye."

"Bye."

As I went back to my room, I felt especially glad to have Jarod as a friend, even if he never wrote when he was away. I thought about how Tina and I would be getting together for lunch again tomorrow, and about how I would be back at work on Monday.

I sat on my bed and stared out the window, at the sky, at the trees. "This," I said out loud, "is going to be a really good summer."

CHAPTER 14

July and August passed quickly, and things were really fun with Tina. We never ran out of stuff to talk about, we just hit it off so well. Sometimes we even had to agree not to talk for an hour or two when we were together so we could just be quiet.

My favorite thing we did over the summer was to have picnics: We'd just lounge around, talking a lot and getting to know each other. We'd try to find spots that were private so we could be physical if we wanted. It still felt really new and scary, and we were going really slowly. Tina was scared, too, which helped me feel better.

Once she had her head in my lap and we were holding hands and talking, and two men walked by. I thought I would die. Tina and I both kind of gave a start, and dropped hands but just stayed where we were and acted like nothing was unusual. They kept walking, but I heard them muttering "dykes" as they walked out of sight. I guess we were lucky they didn't stay and harass us or, god forbid, rape us. It makes me really angry though, that we had to worry about such things.

Tina and I had discussed possibly going on a trip to New York City or Provincetown, Massachusetts to get more of a taste of gay culture. I thought it might help me feel better because I'd never seen any open gay couples before except in a few movies like "La Cage Aux Folles" or something. We hadn't gone on any of those trips yet, but I knew we would at some point.

And we'd done a lot of fun things over the summer: we'd gone hiking several times, swimming, to concerts and lots of movies, and we would just talk about everything. Sometimes we'd get together with Freida and hang out at the gorge. As for our other friends, we hadn't seen the crowd much besides Freida,

because most of them had been away. So now I felt kind of nervous to see them all again: worried they'd figure out what was happening between me and Tina, or that it would feel right to tell them outright but then that they'd drop us as their friends and, at worst, "slander our names" all over school. Tina said she didn't think it would be that bad, but I was still really nervous a lot. Other times I just felt so happy that I didn't care.

Before I knew it, school was about to start up again and then I knew I wouldn't have to "imagine" anymore. I was also psyched about my classes: I'd be taking some advanced biology and environmental sciences courses, so I'd get to go on field trips and just learn a lot. I'd be taking advanced Spanish, too, which I knew I'd love.

Jarod was back, which felt great. I was also looking forward to seeing our other friends regularly again, even if I was nervous about what they might think if they knew Tina and I were lovers!

Tonight my parents were taking Becky and me out to dinner, to "celebrate the end of summer." They also said that once school started tomorrow, they probably wouldn't see as much of us and so they wanted us to all be together tonight. It was a nice gesture on their part, and they were taking us to one of our favorite restaurants, a Chinese food place on the outskirts of town.

I wasn't much looking forward to Becky being there. She'd been kind of snippy all summer since her love life had been really slow. I wondered if maybe she blamed me in some way for her and Bruce not hitting it off, maybe because we were in the same grade or because she guessed I didn't like him. Or maybe, I feared, she suspected about Tina and me and was jealous.

Enough of trying to figure it out, I told myself. I was going to try and enjoy the night.

"Is that what you're wearing?" Mom said, seeing me in my favorite faded blue jeans and a ripped pink teeshirt.

"Yeah. I like these."

"But they're ripped and—"

"Mom…," I said, in my best exasperated tone.

"Okay, okay." My mom shook her head. "I'll back off. I know you're grow-ing up. And I'm basing a character in my new book on you: she wears clothes like you, too…" Her voice trailed off, and her eyes looked faraway. That was my mom all right, always engrossed in her next book.

"Thanks, Mom." At least she wasn't hassling me about what I wore as much anymore. Last year we had a big fight about it one night. When we made up, she agreed she'd try to lay off more and I agreed to make an effort to dress nicer. Maybe I hadn't tonight, but I was glad to see her trying.

I was wondering if maybe I should go put on something dressier when dad and Becky came downstairs.

"Everyone ready?" dad asked.

"Yeah, let's go already," said Becky. "I need to get back early to get ready for school tomorrow."

"Yes ma'am." Dad held the back door open for us and we all went to the car.

"So you're going to be a senior, Sarah. How does it feel?"

Oh no, I thought, dad's putting me in the spotlight again. More lies, more covering up, more talking about everything except the most important thing on my mind.

I tried to think of something I could say. "It feels good, and scary. I don't really want to think about me and my friends all graduating and going our separate ways next June, but I do, even if it is a long way off."

"I know how you feel." Now it was my dad's turn to have a faraway look in his eyes. "I remember feeling that way towards the end of high school, too. But my best friends and I kept in touch."

It's true. Dad still gets cards and letters from a bunch of them and once every couple of years he gets together with one or two of them.

I wished I could tell them about being nervous about going out with Tina and what our friends would think, but I still was no where near ready to tell my family about it.

"How about you, Becky?" said Mom. "Excited?"

I breathed easier now that the focus was on Becky.

"Yeah, I am," she said. "But I'm also worried school will be boring." She picked at her red polished nails.

"How so?" asked dad, as he looked for the turn-off to the restaurant.

Becky listed everything boring about school, about the town, about life. She must really be feeling lonely or something. I was tempted to argue with her, and say what was great about Ithaca and about school, but I sensed she wasn't in the mood to hear it.

When we all got seated in the restaurant, mom and dad started telling us more about stuff they might be working on in the fall: some new stories of mom's, some research projects for my dad. It was neat to know that adults always could do new things in the fall, too, even if they weren't in school.

The meal was nice and spicy, and when the waiter brought out the fortune cookies, we all were excited to see what they said. Becky's said "To err is human, to forgive divine." Dad's said "You will meet a rich woman and marry her."

He said, "Well, that already came true. Your mom is all the riches I could ever need."

"Thanks dear," Mom said, smiling at him. "Mine says 'Find release from your cares, have a good time.' Well, that sounds good to me." She looked so pretty and happy, I felt really glad.

And then finally, I got to open mine. "Fortune will smile on you and your partner."

I smiled, wondering what Tina would say when I told her.

"Oh, that's a nice one," said mom.

"Yeah. Have any lucky man in mind?" dad teased.

"Nope, not right now." I felt really pissed again. It really felt bad, almost like they didn't know anything about me.

Then Becky pointed out, "You spend so much time with Tina, you'd think she was the love of your life."

I practically jumped out of my skin, but I did a pretty good job of hiding it. I had a feeling Becky detected something, though she shut up after that.

"Maybe," I replied calmly, playing it cool as if it was a joke.

Dad didn't seem to notice. "What about your love life, Becky?"

"Still nothing. It's pitiful!"

We all laughed then, even Becky. Then the subject changed back to school and what classes we'd be taking, definitely a relief. I hated having the focus on me and my love life like that, always trying to hide it, always wondering if someone suspected, sometimes half-hoping someone would suspect.

When we got home, Becky and I headed upstairs.

She turned to me. "I know about you and Tina," she whispered to me.

I looked at her. "What are you talking about?"

"You know."

"What are you hinting at, Becky?"

"You're gay, you're gay. Admit it!"

My face got hot. I grabbed her arm and dragged her into my room and slammed the door.

"So what if I am?" I demanded.

"Well, are you?"

"Yes." Then I backed off and went and looked out the window. I practically stopped breathing. I guess I didn't know how she'd take it, and I practically felt nauseous.

Becky stopped cold, too. "You mean, you really are?"

I turned around and faced her. "Yes, I just told you I was." I wanted to take her by her fashionable little curls and shake her, but I settled for just glaring.

"I thought, I mean, I suspected, but I guess I didn't really know."

"Yeah, well now you do know." My fists were clenched and I was practically baring my teeth.

"Hey, I'm sorry, Sarah. It's okay. I mean, it seems strange in a way just because I'm not used to the idea, but I guess I will get used to it. You're still my sister. I'm sorry I was a jerk just now."

I took a deep breath. "Thanks."

"Have you, you know, told anyone? Like do mom and dad know?"

"No. Well, I don't think they suspect, but who knows? And I haven't told them, because I haven't felt ready yet. So please don't mention anything—to them or to anybody." I said the last sentence almost pleadingly.

"Oh, of course not." She seemed to really get how important that was. "And I'm sorry about dinner and my hinting."

"Hey, forget it. If they guess, they guess, or I'll tell them when it feels right. Well, I think I'm going to go call Ms. Tina right now."

"Okay." Becky paused, then asked, "Can I give you a hug?"

I nodded.

We hugged, and to my surprise, I felt tears rolling down my cheeks.

"Hey, do you want to talk more about it?"

I nodded once more, and we sat down on the bed.

"It just feels so hard," I said between sobs. "I always feel like I have to keep it in, that I shouldn't tell most people about my relationship, that I have to pretend I like guys when I like girls and when I'm going out with Tina!"

Becky hugged me again and I cried for another few minutes.

"Oh, Sarah. That must be so hard. I'm really glad you told me, even if I kind of pressured you into it."

We talked for a few minutes more, and she said I could come to her anytime. I felt happy she knew. Now I had two people besides Tina to talk to: Jarod and my sister. And by admitting my gayness outright to Becky, I didn't have to take her little snide comments anymore. Maybe that what she wanted all along: for me to include her. It did feel good to have her know and have her accept me, even if she had called it "strange" at first and needed to get used to the idea. Funny, but to me, being attracted to girls, especially to Tina, felt like the most natural thing in the world.

All in all, I definitely felt good about Becky knowing, and I felt pretty happy as I went to call Tina, my girlfriend.

CHAPTER 15

Tina and I met at the spot we'd agreed upon last night for the first day back at school. We hugged each other hello as any two good friends might, but our eye contact conveyed a love I'd never shared with anyone before.

"It feels so hard to know we won't be able to hold hands or kiss or anything today," I said, nodding in the direction of some other high school couples nearby, walking around arm in arm.

"Yeah, well we'll see," she said, nudging me with her elbow.

The contact felt good. We smiled at each other, then turned and looked at everyone milling around.

"Hey Sarah! Tina!" It was Freida.

"Hey, girl," I said smiling and giving her a hug.

She and Tina hugged too.

"So how does it feel to be a senior?" asked Tina.

"Fantastic! You?"

"Great. It was a really good summer. How was Spain?" Freida had gone with her folks there for the last two weeks.

"Awesome. I practiced my Spanish, and there were a lot of cool kids our age where we stayed, so it was perfect. I even had a boyfriend there. All of the guys were really gorgeous." She looked at us then, and I smiled a little like I understood and supported her. But I didn't say, "Oh, great!" or "Oh, really? Any for me?," like I might have in the past. She stopped talking about it as if sensing that we weren't too excited about it. I guess, for me at least, it was feeling harder for me to fake any sexual interest in guys.

The moment passed though, and we chatted about being back in school and the coming year. It felt good, really good, to talk with her. She was my friend, after all.

Jarod and Sylvia came over soon after, and then Wendell and Abdul. It was just like old times. We made plans to all hang out later since it was a short school day. It felt good to be back.

I got into all the classes I was expecting to, so I was happy with my schedule. It also turned out that Tina and I would be together for Advanced Placement Math, and, more importantly, lunch. I knew that would be fun. Maybe we could even find places to be alone together on some days, even for a little while. I'm sure no one would see us off by the end of the fields or maybe in the little park nearby the school.

I hate this, I thought, clenching my fists. I hated having to hide how I felt about Tina! I just wanted to shout that we were going out. It really pissed me off, and it was only the first day of school.

I got a chance to talk to Tina about it on the way home later, after we'd hung out with the others, when we were walking part of the way home together.

I asked, "Tina, doesn't it bug you that we can't just be open about us and our relationship? Or about being gay, period?"

"You know it bothers me, all the time. It really kills me sometimes. Other times I'm just glad it's not all over school, because I know we could really be harassed by some people."

"I know. Look at what happened at the dance!"

"Yeah, and that was nothing. People get killed and beaten up every day for being gay like us."

"Wow." I'd known that, but I'd never really given it much thought before. I tried to imagine how it would feel to be beaten up, or to see Tina beaten up. I flinched and looked at her. "God, that makes me so mad!" I almost wanted to cry at the thought of it all.

"I know, I know." We walked the next two blocks in silence. Then Tina whispered, "But I'm still happy…to be me, to be a lesbian, I mean, and to have you." And she looked at me tenderly and poked me affectionately in the arm.

I practically melted, and after a quick glance around, I gave her a quick kiss. We both smiled.

"Me too…" I really meant it. "It's worth all the hassles."

We squeezed hands quickly.

"Talk to you tonight?" I said.

"You got it. Around nine?"

"Around nine."

I walked home still feeling the sad and angry feelings and being really happy, all at the same time.

I looked forward to talking to Jarod more about it all, too. I didn't know what I'd do without him. I hoped, too, that I wasn't making him into my therapist, because I certainly was leaning on him. He didn't seem to mind though. And maybe I'd ask Jarod more about what he knew of the "gay scene." Maybe there were even support groups! And Jarod said I could call the college and look into stuff there.

I was getting excited about it all. When I got home, Sylvia had just called. I called her back.

"Hey girl," she said. "Do you want to go to Rebecca's party on Friday night? She told me to tell all of our crowd about it and to invite anyone and everyone." Rebecca had huge parties every so often, whenever her parents were away.

"Yeah, sure, that sounds fun." I coiled the phone cord in my fingers and wondered what it would be like to be at a party with Tina.

"It should be fun, and everyone will be there. Lots of new guys, too. You know how she always knows so many different people."

"Mmm. Well, it'll be good to hang out. Thanks for telling me about it."

We chatted for a while and then got off the phone. I tried to ignore the guy-hunting aspect and just concentrate on how fun it would be to be at a party with everyone, but it was hard.

It definitely seemed like I'd be struggling a lot this year with whether to hide my being gay or not. And I didn't know how well I could hide it.

CHAPTER 16

❀

Rebecca's living room was packed when Tina, Jarod, Gus, and I got to the party. And with Rebecca's parents away, everyone was pretty relaxed. A few people were smoking but it didn't seem that bad.

We all danced in a group.

Gus said, "Hey, Tina, you're a good dancer."

Tina blushed and I laughed. She looked so cute and embarrassed.

We all laughed, joked, and sang loudly to Madonna and the Beatles, the B-52's, and the Go-Go's.

John came over and danced with us. I hoped he wouldn't start flirting with me like he had at the dance last June.

"How're you doing, Sarah? How was your summer?"

'Oh, really good…" I told him briefly about my job and asked him politely about his being a waiter in California, but I really wasn't into talking to him. After a minute or so I just ignored him and paid more attention to Tina, Jarod, and the others. And, like last June, he eventually walked away.

When Tina and I went and sat on the back porch later for a few minutes, she mentioned it.

"John has the hots for you, huh?"

"Yeah, maybe," I laughed. "Not anymore, hopefully."

"He seemed to get the hint after a while."

"Yeah, it feels bad to blow him off and just end the conversation, but I just wasn't into it."

"Yeah, it's okay." She gave my hand a quick squeeze and let go.

I looked in her eyes. I felt the same old joy and the deep anger about having to hide our affection, both at the same time.

Tina seemed to feel the same way, and we looked at each other deeply a moment, then heard the screen door creak open behind us.

"Oh, sorry to interrupt." It was John and one of his friends, Bob. He seemed half pissed and half quizzical. They quickly turned and left.

I gave Tina a look. "Do you think he saw anything?" I whispered.

"I doubt he saw anything blatant; we didn't do anything! Maybe he just picked up the vibes. I hope he doesn't yap about it to everyone." Tina shrugged though.

"I know. I'm scared they'll gossip to everyone and yet another part of me doesn't care. Part of me just wants everyone to know already and be done with it."

We both fumed separately, quietly. Then Sylvia and some other friends came onto the porch.

We talked and joked with them for a while and then went back inside. I tried to forget about my anger at homophobia, my anger at having to hide who I was and my relationship with Tina, but I just couldn't.

Then, to top it off, John walked by me when I was by the refreshment table and asked in my ear, "Are you gay?…" in a long drawl. I glanced at him. He gave me a sinister smile in return and then walked away, going back to laugh with Bob. I turned away and went back and danced with the group, fighting my urges to cry and go smash John's face.

After a while, I couldn't stand it. I turned to Tina.

"I think I'm going to go." I looked away. "Sorry."

Then I said, "Bye Jarod. Bye Freida. Bye everyone." I waved to all my friends and said my pleasantries to Rebecca and a few others. Tina made a motion that we'd talk on the phone in the morning, and she looked worried about me. Also hurt, like why are you leaving so soon? I looked in her eyes and wished I could tell her and just cry, but I couldn't with everyone there, and I just left.

I ran all the way home and didn't notice that it was pouring rain out. I just ran and ran and ran, getting soaked to the skin and feeling like I was going to explode at any second.

CHAPTER 17

I went for several long walks alone that weekend, kicking at rocks and the yellow-red leaves of autumn. I didn't talk much around my family, and I was even quiet around Tina when we studied together on Sunday. She asked if I wanted to talk about it, but I just couldn't.

I had dreams of people with swords with pink triangles on their tips, stalking me and chasing me, and of myself turning around and fighting them with guns, knives, my fists. Sometimes they would win and I would run away, and other times I'd push them over a cliff. Either way, I always woke up shaking.

I lay on my bed Sunday night and thought. I knew I was fighting the pressure to hide being gay, my anger that I had to be careful in this society, my anger at others' homophobia (like John's and Mindy's and Bruce's), and even I still felt a little homophobic deep inside: part of me wished I wasn't gay and wished I didn't have to deal with everything that went with it. Then I felt embarrassed, because I thought I'd gotten through all this before. But that had just been in my head, and now I was really in a relationship and things felt different.

I was sick and tired of hiding who I was and being ashamed of it. I really cared about Tina, maybe even loved her, and here I was so uptight this weekend that I couldn't even talk to her!

I slammed my fist down and pounded my pillow hard, 10, 20, 30 times. Things had to change. I just didn't want to hide who I was anymore.

I went and got the phone and brought it into my room. I dialed information, and I got the number I wanted at the university.

"Gay hotline, please." My heart was pounding.

Then I couldn't stand it. I hung up.

Oh god, I thought. Come on, Sarah.

I waited two minutes, then dialed again. This time, my call went through.

"Hello, gay hotline," I heard a woman's voice say.

I paused. I couldn't speak.

"Hello?" she said again.

My mouth wouldn't move.

I hung up again. What if someone found out it was me and blasted it all over town?

Well, what if they did? Besides, this was a gay hotline. They're gay, too. And they're there to help me, and hotlines always say they're confidential.

I dialed once again.

"Hello, gay hotline," the woman's voice said again.

I took a deep breath. "Yeah, hi. I'm seventeen and I'm lesbian and I guess I just want to talk."

"Great."

"And sorry, but I called a few minutes ago but I…I got scared I guess."

"That's okay, people do it all the time, really."

And so we talked. I told her about when I first knew I was gay, all my attractions, and now my relationship with Tina. I told her about the feeling that I had to hide it from almost everyone and about how angry I felt and how afraid. She let me really rant and rave. And I could tell she was really listening because she'd ask questions to help herself get clear on things I said, or she'd say, "Wow, that sounds hard" or "Yeah, it makes sense you're angry." It felt really good to let it all out and have someone be so supportive.

When I was all done talking, she said, "Wow. Your feelings sound really normal. I've been through a lot of similar experiences and feelings. And it was especially hard for me, too, when I got involved with my first lover. Have you thought about joining any support groups?"

I gulped. "Yes, and I've been afraid. But I think I might be ready. Do you know of any?" I couldn't believe I was actually looking into this.

"Yup. Let's see here." I heard her rustling some papers. "There's the 'Coming Out Support Group, ongoing, Mondays 7:00–8:30.' 'Lesbian social discussion group Wednesdays, 7:00–9:00,' both at the university; and 'Gay, Lesbian, and Bisexual Teens Discussion Group, Sat mornings, 11:00–1:00', downtown."

That was the one. I felt a bit dizzy but tried to keep breathing anyway as I wrote down where it was.

We chatted a bit longer and I got off the phone.

My mind raced. A gay teen group? Who else was gay besides me and Tina?, I wondered. Some kids in town went to the alternative high school, and I bet there were more gay kids there. But that place was real small: they couldn't all be from there. There had to be some more kids from my high school.

I called Tina right away.

"Tina, Tina, guess what?" I yelled, when she picked up the phone.

"What? What?" She said as she laughed at me, and I knew she could tell I'd snapped out of the state I'd been in for the last several days.

"There's a gay teens discussion group over at the community center that meets once a week. Can you believe it? Isn't that great?!"

"Yeah. I know. I actually went there once."

"You did? You're kidding. Why didn't you tell me about it?"

"I guess I sensed you weren't ready before. And it was kind of neat to see you go through your anger phase."

"I sure went through it. I was really pissed this weekend. And I might get pissed again."

"Yeah," she said. "It doesn't ever end, I think."

"What do you mean?"

"Well, we'll always have to deal with whether to come out to people or not, and they'll always be people who hate gays."

"That's for sure."

"And about the discussion group...," she said, "To be honest, I didn't want you to meet some other lesbian and go run off with her."

I drew in a quick breath. Then, calming myself, I gently said, "Oh, Tina, I wouldn't. You know how I feel about you."

"Yeah, yeah, I guess I do know now. I'm sorry I was so insecure."

"That's okay." We chatted a little longer, and we agreed we'd go together to the teen discussion group this coming Saturday. I couldn't wait. And at the end of the conversation, she hesitated. "Hey Sarah?"

"Yeah?"

She paused, then said, "I love you."

My voice cracked. "You do?"

"Yeah."

"Wow. Thanks. I...I think I 'm scared to say it back right now. But I'm glad you said it."

"Really?"

"Yeah. Can I send you a big hug and kiss?"

We both made kissing sounds over the phone. It was the kind of thing I'd always laughed at and been disgusted by when I'd heard other people doing it. I had certainly sworn I'd never do it. Yet feeling so strongly about Tina, it felt nice.

"Mmm...," she said. "And I'm glad you won't say 'I love you' unless you really mean it."

"Thanks. And when it's right, I definitely will say it."

"Good. Well, good night. See you tomorrow."

"Good night."

I felt so good to have Tina as a girlfriend and to be planning to go to the discussion group, that I almost forgot about all the pressures I felt at school and in my family to hide who I really was: a teenage lesbian.

CHAPTER 18

We walked into class the next day, and I couldn't help but look around at everyone and wonder who else could be gay and might be going to the group. Tina said she'd recognized a couple of people from the group at school but that I'd have to see for myself. I think she enjoyed keeping me in suspense.

I realized I hadn't seen Jarod in a while, so I caught up with him between classes and we made plans to go jogging after school.

"Hey, woman, I've missed you," he said when we met at the arranged place. We hugged and then started down the street. We had our special route that we always jogged together, even if it was only once every couple of months.

"You too, man, I've missed you." We laughed.

He told me about the guys and girls he was flirting with nowadays, and I filled him in on how Tina and I were doing, even how she said, "I love you." He said it was natural that sometimes one person is ready to say it sooner than the other. Jarod always knew what to say to help me feel better.

I also told him about the gay teen group I'd be going to.

"Wow," he said. "No kidding? Maybe I'll even come sometime, especially if anything heats up with me and Gus."

"Yeah, that would be neat." That did sound nice, but I felt kind of glad he wouldn't be going for now, though. I really wanted to just go with Tina at first, especially to meet other teen lesbians to compare feelings and experiences with.

"You know, Sarah, I think a lot of people are catching on to you and Tina."

"You're kidding!" Even though I knew it was true, I stared at him, half horrified and half excited. "Who?"

"Well, Mindy and Bruce, of course, for starters."

I made a face. "Those two would harass anyone who's not glued to the opposite sex."

"True, but I'm glad they haven't caused you any trouble this term."

"Mmm. So who else knows?" I looked at the trees while we kept jogging.

"Well, I heard John talking again…"

"Oh yeah." I looked over at Jarod. "He let me know he sensed 'the energy' between me and Tina at Rebecca's party. And I discouraged his interest in me first, so he's probably pissed."

"Probably. Wendell and Abdul also casually mentioned to me that they wondered when you and Tina were going to find boyfriends. I don't think they definitely think you're gay, but I get the impression it's crossed their minds."

"Wow. What did you say?"

"Oh, just that you were very selective. And they let it drop. I don't think they'll bring it up again, but they'd probably be accepting if they knew."

"That's good." I felt kind of weird about the whole conversation. I had a feeling I'd be more upset later on, but for right at that moment, a weird calm came over me.

Jarod and I jogged for a while in silence. I kicked a pinecone out of the way and looked at the leaves turning colors on the trees. So people were starting to catch on. It felt wild and yet it also made sense. After all, how could Tina and I hide it even if we tried to be careful? We spent so much time together that even if we weren't gay, people would suspect we were. And I wondered who else had figured it out or suspected besides the ones Jarod and I knew about.

My fear was creeping up again, and I tried to forget about it. Jarod and I identified some birds (he was interested in birds, too, but not as much as me), and we joked about some of our teachers. We made fun of Mrs. Hendricks, the math teacher with her droopy face and droopy voice, and of Ms. Samuels, the music appreciation teacher who said, "Now children, call me Barbara, but don't tell the principal!" Actually, we kind of liked her and thought she was cool. And Jarod told me about his sister's bizarre sculptures that were being shown in the gallery on State Street. It was a really nice jog, all in all.

After saying our goodbyes, I walked home slowly to wind down. I thought of the math test I had to study for, about the Shakespeare paper I needed to start writing, and about Tina.

I ate my mom's hamburger dinner with my family quickly, then did my homework and studied till 11:00 p.m. I didn't want to think about lots of people probably knowing about Tina and me, but I had a feeling I wouldn't be able to escape my worrying.

And I was right, because I had another scary dream, this one a real nightmare. Tina and I were in a classroom: it was biology, and Ms. Samuels was teaching it. All our friends were there and all the people Jarod had said knew about my relationship. I wondered why Ms. Samuels wasn't teaching music appreciation. I stood up and said, "Hey Barbara, what do you know about biology?" She turned quickly, and with a gleam in her eye, pointed a purple, nail-polished finger and said, "I know what *you* know about biology. Ha ha ha ha ha," and she started cackling in a horrible laugh, and everyone else in the class started pointing and laughing, too. Tina shrank to the size of a dust speck and ran into my lap, saying, "Help me, help us. They'll KILL us!" I said, "There, there, it doesn't matter. It doesn't matter what they think. We'll graduate and then we'll never see them again." Meanwhile, they began pelting us with bibles and some couples came towards us with their arms around each other and said, "We're straight," and "We're normal, why aren't you?"

I woke up. It was 4:00 a.m.

The old fear was back with me. I knew people would realize more and more that Tina and I were a couple, and that there was probably nothing I could do about it if I wanted to be who I really was, a lesbian. Plus I knew there was a part of me that wanted them to know, too. I was starting to feel that their knowing outright would be the best thing.

I figured maybe I needed to use reverse psychology: don't even try to hide it. Maybe if someone called me gay to my face, I should just admit it and have an attitude of, "So what?," like I did with Becky. Then people might respect me and my sexuality more. Since it seemed like there was nothing I could do about them knowing at this point, I decided I might as well not try to cover it up. I wanted to act proud of it, because that was how I really felt in my heart.

By 6:00 a.m., I decided to get up and go watch birds for a while, since I couldn't sleep. I was looking forward to seeing Tina at school, and I was really excited about the gay discussion group on Saturday. I deserved to be gay and happy, and I was going to start right now.

CHAPTER 19

"Go in first," I said.

"No, you go in first."

I walked in, having no idea what my first gay teen discussion group would be like. My whole being wanted to both shout with joy and run far, far away.

There were four guys and three girls there already, and three more people came in after we did. I even recognized one guy from my and Tina's math class.

"Hi, Sarah," he said, his eyes opened wide. Then his expression faded into a warm smile and he added, "Nice to see you here."

"Thanks. I…I'm surprised to see you here, too. I guess I had no idea what to expect. Do you two know each other?," I asked him and Tina.

"Not really. Hi, I'm Tina," she said.

"Hi. I'm Craig." He shook Tina's hand. "I'm not as surprised about you two," he said to us.

"Really? How?" I asked.

"Via Mindy Mallory I think. It's terrible, but those rumors spread."

Tina and I both nodded, knowingly.

Before we had a chance to talk more, another guy started leading the group. We all introduced ourselves and they all said how long they'd been coming to the group and what they'd gotten out of it. Many said they felt better about being gay, less alone, more able and willing to look for a lover if they didn't already have one, and that they had made friends in the group.

Then we all shared some of our coming out stories, since that was this weekend's scheduled topic.

The discussion leader hadn't known until he got a crush on his best friend, who also turned out to be gay. His lover was there, too, and he said he'd just found out when they'd met. Later both had realized they'd been gay all along but had pushed down the thoughts. We all nodded knowingly. One girl said she'd been attracted to one of her mother's friends a few years ago, and then had fallen for an older girl she knew. She still hadn't been in a relationship with a woman, but she knew she was a lesbian and was no longer interested in guys. She said most guys seemed to just sense that she just wanted to be friends and treated her more naturally and flirted with her less now.

Another girl and guy both said they were bisexual: attracted to both sexes, but even if they were involved in a heterosexual relationship they would still want a support group because of who they were inside. And their girlfriends or boyfriends were usually fine with them being "bi," as long as they were loyal to them during the relationship.

Two other guys were feeling unsure or upset about being gay: they'd just recently gotten involved and heard about the group. Another guy was single now but had known he was gay for a long time, like me.

One of the last women, Page, had only decided she was a lesbian the year before but was now very "out" at the alternative school and in some adult gay rights group. Her girlfriend, Cynthia, was just starting to come out since they got involved six months ago.

All in all, it was really exciting to be there. I felt like jumping up and down, it was so great.

In the next three weeks, we were going to talk about gays in the media, coming out to our parents, and coming out to friends. I knew *I* could certainly use those topics.

And Tina and I and Cynthia and Page agreed to get together later that night to go to a movie—I couldn't wait! Our first double date.

Tina and I left and then went our separate ways for the afternoon. We both had some studying to do, and I'd promised dad I'd be home for dinner to taste a new recipe he was trying. Tina and I would get together again at around 8:30 to meet Cynthia and Page for the movie.

I was psyched that we'd finally be going out with another lesbian couple, and I was smiling and whistling as I entered my house to go study.

CHAPTER 20

Mom, dad, and Becky were sitting in the living room looking sad when I came in. I knew something was wrong.

"What is it?"

"It's grandma," said mom, and I saw her face was red and blotchy. "She died this morning."

"Oh no." I sat down with them, feeling a bit numb. "When...? What happened?"

"This morning. A heart attack. Uncle Harry and Aunt Joanne are taking care of the arrangements. I figured we'd all drive there in the morning." Mom's brother Harry and his wife Joanne and their kids all lived in Binghamton, not far from grandma's nursing home.

"I can't believe it. I'm going to miss her so much." Even though I hadn't seen her in a few months, it always had felt so good to know she was there.

"Yeah, we'll all miss her," dad said sadly. I knew he would. Even though she was mom's mother, he still called her "mom," too.

Becky kept crying a lot. "Why did she have to die? Why does anyone have to die?" she sobbed. I felt bad for her. She was taking it really hard. I was, too, but I don't think it had hit me yet.

We all hung out and talked about how we felt and what we remembered. It helped me feel a little less sad. Then I went up to my room; I needed to be alone.

All I could do was think about grandma. Since I wasn't able to get any of my math and history done, I decided to call Tina.

"Hi, cutie," she said, when she heard my voice. "Is everything okay for tonight?"

"Yeah, it's fine. It's just that…" My voice cracked and I started crying. "My grandmother died."

"Oh Sarah. I'm so sorry. When did it happen?"

I gave her the brief rundown. It helped to just tell her everything and cry. Then I had an idea.

"Hey, Tina, would you want to come with me, I mean, with us, to the funeral? I'd really love it if you could be there."

"Wow, I didn't even think of going. Yeah, sure. So I'd go there in the same car as you and your family?"

"Yeah. I'll have to ask my parents, but I think it'll be okay."

"So when is the funeral?"

"Some day next week, I guess. I'll let you know."

"Okay…And are you sure you're still up for going out tonight?"

"Yeah, it'll be good to see you and to have some fun with Page and Cynthia. It'll get my mind off grandma…" I could tell my voice sounded really sad.

"Well, I send you a hug. I'm really sorry again about your grandma."

"Thanks. And thanks for the hug."

"Okay, see you later."

We hung up, and I was able to cry a little more. I was really glad I had called Tina.

Then I started to worry about what my parents would say about bringing Tina to the funeral. I decided to go get it over with.

My mom was staring off into space in front of her typewriter when I went into her study.

She looked up. "Oh, hi honey."

"Hi." I put my arm around her and now *she* cried a little. It felt weird to see my mom so sad, and yet I was glad I could support her. Then I cried again a little.

"It feels scary to be an orphan," she said finally. Her father had died two years before, and she'd also taken that pretty hard. "And I know it's hard for you, too, honey."

"Yeah, we can all be sad together."

We were quiet for a minute. I was also thinking of her and dad dying someday and me being an orphan. I gave a quick shudder, then said "I hope you and dad live a long time."

She smiled at me and stroked my hair. "I do, too." After a minute, she added, "Did you just come in to spend some time, or was there something else specific on your mind?"

"Well, both, actually." I paused. "I was wondering if it'd be okay with you if Tina came with me to the funeral."

"Your friend Tina? Sure, honey, if you want your friend there."

"Thanks, mom." I kissed her on the cheek.

"Is she your best friend now?"

I blushed and looked away for a second. "Yeah, I guess you could say that."

"Well, that 's good, Sarah. It's nice to have a best friend."

I nodded, feeling heavy in my chest that I hadn't told her everything.

"Anyway, don't stay out too late tonight, okay?"

"I won't." I kissed her again. "See you later."

There, I thought. That was easy enough. And I was glad I could be support-ive to mom. And now didn't feel at all like the time to come out to her, and yet I hoped the time would be *soon*.

Now to ask dad.

"Hey pop." I knocked on his door. He was reading.

"Hey. Come on in. How're you doing?"

"Okay. Sad…"

"Yeah, me too. Your grandmother was a special lady." He looked at me, smiled gingerly, and held my hand.

"Yeah. And, um, dad? I already checked with mom, but I wanted to ask you, too, if I could bring my friend Tina to the funeral?"

"Tina? Oh sure. Invite whomever you want. But only one can fit in the car with us."

"Yeah, it'll just be her."

"Okay, fine."

"Well, I've got to go work on my homework before I go out tonight."

"With Tina?"

As always, I wondered if he was catching on.

"Yeah, with Tina and two other girls." I wanted to change the subject. "So are you still making that recipe tonight?"

"I'm not sure. I'll have to decide if I'm up for it. But I'll make something for dinner, in any case."

"Good," I said, "See you later."

"Okay, bye."

Part of me felt guilty for even mentioning bringing a friend when everyone felt so sad. I also tried to remember that I was sad, too, and deserved to have my girlfriend be there with me.

And I felt really glad Tina would be able to come. I tried not to think of what my parents or any relatives might guess or think about us. And I tried to get excited, despite my sadness, for the double date tonight.

CHAPTER 21

"So how're you doing, kiddo?" Tina put her arm around me and held me for a long time. We were in her room, hanging out for a few minutes before going to meet Cynthia and Page.

After several minutes, we let go, and I wiped the tears out of my eyes. "Wow, I can't believe how sad I feel, I've never had anyone close to me die before."

"Yeah, I know. It's hard. I was really shaken up when my grandfather on my dad's side died last year."

"Really?" I said slowly. "I didn't remember you were close to him." We had discussed our grandparents before, but she hadn't seemed like she'd been close to any of them.

"I wasn't, but still, I loved him a lot and it shook me up."

"Hmm. Well, I'm sorry about him, too."

"Thanks," she said. "I can tell you more about him another time; we should get going or we'll be late."

"Yeah. You're right. Let's go."

"Are you sure you'll be okay for tonight?," she asked, putting her arm around me.

"Yeah. I'm sad, but I'm also psyched to get together with them."

"Me too, and nervous."

"Yeah, our first double date."

"Mmm." We gave each other a quick kiss and squeezed hands before we headed out the door, entering our new social life as part of the gay community.

CHAPTER 22

❀

We met Cynthia and Page outside the movie theater as planned.

The line was pretty long, so it gave us a good chance to all talk together and get to know each other. We talked about our schools, our families, movies we'd seen recently (especially ones with cute women), sports, and hiking. Anyone hearing us or seeing us would've thought we were just any bunch of four girls hanging out on a Saturday night. But it felt great to know the truth.

Cynthia and Page made a cute couple: Cynthia had straight brown shoulder length hair and brown eyes and a medium build. She was pretty soft spoken, but she said she was learning to speak up, especially because she had big breasts and guys were constantly coming on to her. Page had short curly blond hair, and she was short and a bit stocky. She looked pretty tough in her second-hand leather jacket.

In the theater, we all joked a little, in very low voices, about all the straight couples. It was really funny. We did it by playing telephone, Cynthia whispering in Page's ear, Page in Tina's, and Tina in mine, so no one could hear us. It was fun, and it felt great being out with other people besides Tina who knew what it was like to be a lesbian teenager, to feel so left out of what most people at school were into and to always feel pressure to hide who we were.

The movie was a comedy and really funny. Tina and I held hands, which felt nice, especially with Cynthia and Page beside us doing the same.

When the movie ended, Page said, "I know this isn't politically correct, but how's about going to Jack's, the gay bar?"

"You're kidding!" I couldn't believe it. "There's no way they'd let us in. We're obviously not of drinking age."

"True," she said. "But sometimes, if the person at the door isn't into the age-ist thing, they'll let us in anyway."

"She's right," said Cynthia. "They've let us in sometimes and we've had a lot of fun." She quickly squeezed Page's shoulder.

"Really?" I said, looking at Tina. I couldn't believe it. I'd never even consid-ered going in there, and I guess Tina never mentioned it either because she hates drinking or because she didn't know about it either.

"Yeah," said Tina. "I'd heard that, and I tried to get in once, before I met you, Sarah, but they practically laughed me away. So obviously I never tried again."

"That makes me so angry," said Page. "The men can be sexist and rude about it. Then again, some are really nice, and if a woman is checking i.d.'s along with him, she might help us out. It's worth a try if you two are up for it."

"Well, what do you say, sweetie?" Tina poked me in the ribs, our favorite public way of affectionate touching.

"Sure. I'm game."

We headed towards the bar, all of us walking quietly now. It was a beautiful night, bright and clear. We could see lots of stars, even from the well-lit street, and I could hear dogs barking off in the distance.

I started to feel sad again, about grandma. Tina noticed and gave my hand a quick squeeze.

Cynthia and Page saw the look pass between us, so I figured I should explain.

"If I'm a little out of it tonight, it's because I just found out this afternoon that my grandmother died."

"Oh, Sarah. I'm really sorry." Page seemed really empathetic.

"Yeah, that's rough." Cynthia looked concerned. "Is there anything we can do?"

"No, thanks. It helps just to be out and having fun, to get my mind off it."

"Well, feel free to be sad. I know how hard it is," said Page. "Be as sad and party-pooperish as you want."

"Thanks." I couldn't help laughing.

We got to the gay and lesbian bar, and lo and behold, the guy at the entrance let us in. He was a broad, tall, tough-looking man, and he just winked at us and said, "Just don't order any drinks, okay?"

"Gotcha," said Page. We all went in and stood along a wall until we could adjust to the light and get a good view of what was happening.

There were a lot of people there. The place wasn't too big, but the dance floor was jammed with gay men and lesbians. I just couldn't believe it; it was great. There were tons of female couples and male couples, women holding hands and kissing, men holding hands and kissing. The couples were holding each other, looking openly into each other's eyes, dancing regularly in pairs and large groups, and just hanging out and talking. It blew me away. I'd hardly ever seen any openly gay couples in my life, and here were dozens. I also felt self-conscious for some reason.

We all just stood around and watched for a long while. It was so neat just to be there. We were definitely by far the youngest ones there, and a few people cast curious glances in our direction. One guy, walking by with his lover, even said, "Hi, kids—welcome to Jack's," in a friendly way. But mostly no one paid us any special attention, which was good.

After a while, Cynthia and Page started towards the dance floor.

"You two coming?" Cynthia called over her shoulder.

"Shall we, my sweet?" Tina said, taking my hand.

"I'm still in shock." I looked in her eyes. "Is it really okay to dance together, the way we really want to dance together?" I rubbed her hand.

"It sure looks like it's safe," she said, smiling.

We hugged for a full minute, then I took a deep breath, nodded, and walked with Tina onto the dance floor.

And it was great. I forgot my sadness for a while and just got into the music, the dancing, and the great company. It felt so freeing to just be able to dance with women and be gay, and to dance with my lover, Tina. I felt so glad there was this safe space.

We left by midnight, as we were all getting tired. Tina and I kissed good night before we left the place, and the rest of us all hugged good-bye.

"Will we see you two women at the discussion group next week?," Page asked.

"You bet. I'll be there. Will you, Tina?"

"I'm planning to. And it was great getting together with you two. We'll have to do it again."

"Yeah." I agreed.

"I'd like that," said Cynthia.

"Definitely," said Page.

"Well, see you Saturday morning then," I said. "Bye."

Tina and I walked partly home together, agreeing we had both had fun with our two new friends.

It had been a great evening, and I knew the upcoming funeral would be a whole different kind of gathering.

CHAPTER 23

"Is everyone ready?" asked dad. Tina and I were sitting on the sofa chatting with Becky, and mom was in the kitchen packing some snacks for the trip.

"Coming," yelled mom, and we all got up and headed for the car.

It felt funny to see everyone in black, especially mom and Becky who both like to dress in bright colors. In fact, I wanted to burst into hysterical laughter. Sometimes I held it in; other times it just erupted out of me and I couldn't help it. My family knew I was really sad, which makes me sometimes want to laugh. I'm glad they understood and didn't get mad.

Otherwise, we were all pretty quiet during the drive. Usually my parents are very sociable with my friends and would get into a lively discussion about something or other; in fact, they had talked with Tina a couple of times before and seemed to like her a lot. But today, it was understood that they weren't in a talking mood, which was okay with all of us. After all, it's hard to make small talk when a close family member has just died.

We settled down for the long drive. It felt really hard to not be able to hold Tina's hand openly. We did for a few minutes under my coat, since I knew Becky wouldn't care if she saw, but I just wasn't willing to have my parents see anything from the front seat and have to tell them about us, and about me, right then. Still, it would've been nice to have been able to be comforted by Tina more during the ride.

We got to Binghamton in an hour, got out, and stretched. Other cars were pulling up, too, with my cousins, aunts, and uncles, and with friends of my grandmother.

My uncle Harry came right over. "Oh, Betsy, I'm so glad you're here."

"Oh, Harry." Mom choked on her words and cried a little in his arms. When they were done, Uncle Harry hugged dad, then came over and hugged me and Becky. we don't usually all hug, but it just felt right. It was different because of what had called us all together today.

Then I did introductions. "Uncle Harry, this is my friend, Tina. And Tina, this is my Uncle Harry." They shook hands.

"Nice to meet you, Tina."

"Nice to meet you, too."

I obsessed a little bit about what Uncle Harry thought of me bringing a friend and if he suspected anything. I realized, though, that no one really cared, they were too busy being sad.

Then I noticed some of my cousins I hadn't seen in a while. "Tina, I'm going to go say hi to some other relatives. Do you mind if I leave you for a few minutes?"

"Oh, no, it's fine. I'll just wander around a little."

I went over to my cousins Mary and Christina.

"Sarah!"

We all hugged and clung together, and I could see tears in both their eyes.

"Oh, Sarah, I'm so glad you're here," said Christina.

"And I'm glad you two are here. I can't believe grandma's dead."

"I know, I know," said Mary.

Even though we didn't see each other that often, we had always been close, especially Christina and I.

"How have you been, Sarah?" Christina squeezed my arm.

"Good, really good, except for this, you know, being sad. I hope we get to talk more after the funeral."

"I'm sure we'll get time at the reception," said Christina. "Looks like everyone is going in."

"Oh, right. Well, I'll talk to you all later, then," and we hugged again.

I went back to Tina, and I was looking forward to introducing her to everyone later. She was chatting with a distant cousin of mine. I was glad Tina wasn't bored or didn't feel out of place, at least not obviously.

We went in and joined my family up front.

Mom leaned over Becky and whispered to me, so Tina couldn't hear, "Do you think it's appropriate for her to sit up here with the closest family members of the dead person?"

I felt my face turning red, and I wanted to both slide under the bench and also take my mom's pocketbook and slug her with it.

Becky heard and spoke up, thank god. "Oh mom. Loosen up. She brought a friend to comfort her."

And I said, "Yeah, mom. I didn't mean to upset you. I just thought she could sit here with me. I—"

We were interrupted by the minister starting to speak. I'm glad Tina got to be next to me. If she were a guy and my boyfriend, I wondered if mom would have said anything. And I knew if Tina was a guy and my boyfriend, we'd be holding hands openly, maybe she'd even have her arm around me. That, as usual, pissed me off that we couldn't express our affection in public. We did sit close together, and she did put her hand on my shoulder a few times, which helped a lot.

I cried a bit during the ceremony as they talked about grandma's life and what she was like. I could hear Becky crying, too, next to me, and I reached over and held Becky's hand at least. After a while, Tina took my other hand. I was nervous at first, but then I realized that's what any set of female friends would do at a time like this, so I relaxed. Mom must have been all cried out already since she was being pretty quiet, with her head on dad's shoulder.

After it was over, we all kind of sat there, soaking it all in.

"Well," said mom, after a minute, "that was certainly a beautiful ceremony."

"Yeah, it was," I agreed. We all stood up finally.

"So she's being cremated, right mom?" Becky asked.

"Yes. That's what she wanted. So we're just going to go to Uncle Harry's for the reception."

We headed for the door. Everyone around us was walking slowly and crying and hugging. I waved at a few more relatives but we didn't make any move to talk; I think everyone was wiped out from the ceremony.

Tina was nearby throughout all this, being quietly supportive. It felt really nice. One or two distant aunts came over to hug my mom, and they were glancing at Tina, wondering who she was. Probably they figured she must be a friend of mine. I wasn't going to worry too much about it.

We got back in the car for the short drive.

"I wish she were going to be buried in the cemetery," Becky burst out. "I can't believe she wanted her body burned up into ashes!," and she started crying again.

We were all kind of quiet. Then Tina said, "I know how you feel. My grandfather got cremated. I felt horrible. I mean, I loved him so much, even though we weren't close, and it was hard to think of his body being burned into ashes. It was terrible." Tina had a faraway look in her eyes. "Then after about a year, I came to accept it and even feel good about his ashes being scattered on his favorite hill where he wanted."

Becky seemed heartened a bit by that. "Thanks." She gave Tina a little smile and looked a little less sad.

We rode the rest of the way quietly and then pulled up near Uncle Harry's. Tina and I said we wanted to get some air,so we lingered outside and walked around the block.

"How you doing, partner?" Tina poked me gently.

"Okay." I looked at her deeply. I think I began to really love her at that moment. "Sad." And I started to cry. We were way out of sight from the house and I was glad; Tina gave me a big, long hug and I even sobbed a little. "Thanks for coming today, it must not be thrilling to be at a funeral or have to deal with tons of my family members you don't know."

"Hey, Sarah. It's okay. I want to be here with you. You're my lover, remember? I love you, whether you like it or not."

"Oh, yeah, I forgot." We laughed.

I looked around, no cars were near, and no one else seemed to be in the street. I leaned over and I kissed her.

"You know," I said hesitatingly. "I think I love you, too. And I want to say that not only when someone just died, but all the time. And I think I will. I…I love you."

Tina looked at me lovingly as I said all this, then quickly kissed me. "I'm glad. And I'm glad you could say it. I—"

A window from the house right in front of us slammed shut, and we could see a woman angrily looking at us as she quickly shut her blinds. We looked at each other again and chuckled.

"Oh well," said Tina, shrugging.

"Yeah, it's our old friend, homophobia." We rolled our eyes and headed back towards the house for the reception. It pissed me off what that woman had done, but that was her business. I wondered if she'd say something to Uncle Harry next time she saw him, like "Were those two girls I saw kissing each other on the street part of that funeral reception you had?" But no, she probably didn't even know Uncle Harry, and even if she did, she couldn't know we were necessarily going to his house.

In any case, if the relatives were going to figure out who my "friend" was, so be it. I was there to grieve my grandmother's death, and I was glad Tina was with me.

CHAPTER 24

❁

"Christina, I want you to meet my friend, Tina."

Christina looked at her warmly, even though Christina's eyes were puffy from crying. And her shoulder length blond curls were frizzier than usual. I still loved her: Christina was great.

"Nice meeting you, Tina."

"Likewise."

"That's so great that you could come and be with Sarah today. I didn't even think to ask anyone," she said sadly.

"Yeah, well, I wish it was a happier occasion. And I'm sorry about your grandmother."

"Thanks. Sarah here helped me through it this morning." Christina hugged me around the waist.

"Yeah," I said. "This is my favorite cousin."

Christina blushed. "Aw, shucks...So do you two go to the same school and all?"

"Yup," said Tina. "The same classes, interests, shirt size."

Christina giggled.

"We were drawn to each other, like mice to cheese, it was meant to be."

I was glad Tina was hamming it up, and I felt uncomfortable at the same time. Little did Christina know Tina was serious!

And yet little did I know. Christina crept up behind me later and asked to go for a walk. I waved to Tina that I was going out; she was engaged in a conversation with my Uncle Dave about colleges or something and nodded.

Christina and I went walking around the neighborhood, past where Tina and I had gone. We just walked and walked and looked at the leaves changing colors. The wind was blowing hard and we could hear the leaves bristling in the cool fall air. They were a beautiful mixture of reds, yellows, greens, and browns.

We talked about grandma and some favorite memories of ours, like the time she'd told us all those stories about Russia, where she grew up, and about the time we cousins all stayed at her house for a week when our parents all went on a trip together. Laughing a lot, we remembered how we'd all run around playing tag in the house; grandma was so upset she practically tore her hair out. Finally she'd yelled, "Outside! And I'm 'it'!" So we'd all ran outside and she chased us around the backyard until she was too tired to run anymore. We knew she wasn't really mad anymore and we'd all gone inside and had hot chocolate.

"Wow," I said. "It feels so fun to talk with you. It's been such a long time."

"I know. We should call each other more. So what do you do for fun up in Ithaca nowadays?"

"Oh, the usual: lots of bird watching, hiking, spending time with my friends like Tina, Jarod, and others, going to the discos...How about you?"

"I'm doing my dancing a lot." Christina's passion was modern and jazz dancing. "I'm still taking classes, and I'm choreographing the dances for this semester's school play."

"That's great."

"Yeah. I can hardly believe it. And other than that, it's been a good time lately, lots of social stuff. Did I tell you about my new boyfriend, Bob?"

"No. And I haven't met him? How do I know he's honorable?"

"He just is, dummy!" She giggled. I loved to make her laugh.

"Well, what's he like?"

"Oh, he's really nice and open, very tall, blond hair, funny. He's into chemistry and physics, and he wants to be a research scientist. And he's one of the dancers in the school show. That's how I met him last year, in a play."

"Great."

We walked along in silence some more. "So...uh, how about you? Any love life?" She looked me in the eye.

"Hmm. Kind of. Nothing worth mentioning." Inside I was fighting with myself. I really wanted to tell her about Tina and I, and yet I was really scared she'd think it was gross or something.

"Sarah, can I ask you something? Are you gay? I mean, are you and Tina more than friends?" I was shocked. Part of me wanted to lie and say no, but I couldn't.

"Yes." I barely whispered it, and I kept my eyes on the ground. I almost sounded angry to myself, I was so afraid she wouldn't like me anymore. I looked up at her then.

"Sarah." she said. "I'm really glad you told me. I didn't know if you were or not, I was just wondering, because you never talked about guys ever, so I just took a risk and guessed. I was scared that maybe you weren't and would think I was crazy or would hate me, but I feel so close to you, I just wanted to ask. I think it's great."

I gave her a big hug. "Thanks, Christina. That means a lot. I get really scared to tell people, as you might guess."

"Yeah, I can imagine." She put her arm around me and we hugged again. "It must be really hard."

"Yeah." I wiped a tear from my eye.

"And I think it's really brave of you to have brought Tina today. I was afraid to even bring Bob. You know, is it appropriate at grandma's funeral, what will my relatives think of him, maybe he won't want to come. All that stuff."

"Really? I thought only I went through all those worries because I was gay."

"No, we all go through it. Then again, you do have it harder, because I'm sure a lot of people would look down on your relationship. Look at Aunt Carol. She's always making homophobic comments, racist comments, elitist remarks. I bet it would be hard to come out to her."

"Yeah, it would be like an invitation for her wrath." I made my voice high-pitched. "'Ooh, Sarah, I never knew you engaged in such disgusting practices.' Just the thought of her saying it makes me sick."

"Especially since she probably wouldn't say it directly to you, but would just have a disgusted look on her face." Then she said, "Well, again, I'm glad you decided to tell *me*," and we gave each other a warm, tight hug.

We headed back inside, catching up on other stuff. It felt good to feel close to her and not have to hide anything. I hoped that with my parents, too, I could soon do the same.

CHAPTER 25

I called Tina on the phone as soon as we got home. We hadn't really had anymore alone time the rest of the day. "So what did you really think of today, of the whole funeral and everything?"

"It was okay, really. I liked your family. Everyone seemed nice."

"Really?"

"Yeah. Your Uncle Dave was nice. Are you sure he's not gay?"

I laughed. "Yeah, I'm sure. He just got divorced from his wife two years ago, and he has a girlfriend last I heard. But who knows? Maybe he's bisexual, or repressed. Anyway, so who else did you talk to?"

"Oh, Mary and Christina a bit. They were really friendly. I can see why you're so close with both of them, especially Christina."

"I'm glad you liked her. And guess what?"

"What?"

"I came out to her and told her about us and everything!"

"Really?! How was it?"

"She was so supportive. And she asked me if I was gay; I didn't even have to bring it up myself. She just wanted me to be honest. It was scary, but then I felt so much closer to her afterwards."

"Great. I don't think any of my family would want to know. They'd just want to ignore it or convert me back to being straight."

"Yeah, me too. I'm looking forward to that rap group on the subject."

"Um. So, you must still be so sad about your grandmother."

"Yeah, I am." I took a deep breath. I said slowly, "And I guess I will be for a while. The funeral helped though, to hear about her life and to share with people. I guess that's why it's good to have funerals."

"Good. I'm glad it helped."

I cleared my throat. "And I just wanted to say, again, that I love you."

"Aw…I still love you, too."

My heart was doing flip-flops. "See you at school, okay?"

"Yeah, bye."

It was still hard for me to say, "I love you" to Tina, but it sure was getting easier.

CHAPTER 26

❀

I lay down on my bed later that night and put on some classical music. I some-times found that kind of music depressing, but I was starting to think about grandma again and I just wanted something mellow.

I wondered again if grandma still would have loved me if she knew I was gay. Yes, I had to believe she would have—I just had to. I thought about the time grandma gave us all breakfast in bed for Christmas, when she and grandpa had stayed over that year.

I noticed my tears were getting my pillow all wet, but I didn't care. I couldn't stop crying, and I was making loud sobbing noises.

Becky must have heard me because she knocked on my door. "Sarah? Are you okay?"

"Oh. Come on in." I felt a little embarrassed and then decided what the heck, I might as well not be alone with it.

She saw me crying and came over and held me. "About grandma?"

"Yeah." And I sobbed some more.

"I know, I know. I'm sad, too." And then Becky started crying.

"Do you remember the breakfasts in bed?"

"Yeah." She was quiet for a while and we both thought about it. "Or the time we all went to the amusement park near Albany?"

"Oh, yeah, I hadn't thought about that in a while. Remember how she prac-tically fell over the counter trying to knock those cans down to win us a stuffed animal?"

I smiled. "Yeah…Or when she and grandpa clung to each other for dear life on the roller coaster?"

"Oh my god! I was afraid they'd both have a heart attack, the way she was screaming." We were both laughing by now, even though we were still wiping tears from our eyes.

"And how she swore she'd never set foot in another ride again, but then went in the haunted house with us and screamed some more?"

We had a good time remembering stories and tidbits of things she'd said and done.

"You know," I said, "this is what we need more of at funerals. To be able to laugh at the good times."

"I know."

We chatted for a few more minutes and then said good night.

There are definitely sometimes benefits to having a sister!

CHAPTER 27

"So the rap topic for today is 'Coming Out to Our Parents.'"

We all took turns leading the group, and today was Page's turn. Cynthia, Tina, and the other regulars were all there.

I swallowed hard. I'd been feeling more and more like I didn't want to hide my sexuality from my folks, and yet I was scared to death to tell them.

"I asked to lead today's rap," Page continued, "because as many of you know, I came out to my parents a few months ago and I need to talk about it. Plus maybe my experience can help someone else."

"So what happened when you told them? What did you say?" I couldn't help prodding her along.

"Well, I just couldn't stand it anymore. After all, Cynthia and I had been going out for a while. Finally, after one time of teasing and heterosexist pressure from my folks about when I would get a boyfriend, I just had to tell them. So I just blurted out, 'I'm gay'.

"And what happened?" asked someone.

"Then I added, 'I know you might hate me, but I need to be honest.'"

We all leaned forward, waiting for more.

"They stared at me, then looked at each other. My mom said, 'Are you sure?' My dad said, 'You must be kidding; you're only seventeen.' I told them, 'Yes, I'm sure. Cynthia and I are lovers.' My dad slapped me in the face and stormed out of the house. My mom said, 'Are you all right?' When I nodded, she said, 'Well, let's talk about this later. I don't think your father and I are too happy about this.' And she went upstairs. It was horrible." Her voice cracked.

We were all quiet for a little while.

Then I asked, "How have they been since then?"

"My dad hasn't spoken to me. My mom has been cold and civil, though she seems to be loosening up a bit in the past week. She even asked me if I wanted her to cook my favorite meal when relatives come over next week. But she hasn't mentioned my being gay and neither has my father."

We were all quiet again for a long minute. After a while, Cynthia spoke.

"I guess I've been lucky, even though I'm still pissed at my folks. I told my parents last year, and even though they say, 'You're young. Maybe you'll change your mind when you're older,' both of them have also said, 'We're not thrilled but we still love and accept you.'"

"That is pretty good," said Page, and no one argued.

"Of course ideally, we'd all like them to say, 'Good for you, whatever makes you happy, we'll march with you in a gay pride parade.' But I guess that's rare."

Cynthia had a point there. That was a lot to expect. And part of me felt guilty because I had a sense that my parents would be fairly accepting, at least as accepting as Cynthia's, if not more. But that still wasn't helping me tell them. I knew I wanted my parents to know, but I was petrified.

We all discussed the pros and cons of coming out in different ways and at different times, if at all. A lot of the others weren't out to their parents either, but it was good to hear everyone' experiences who had. I felt better knowing I wasn't the only one who was afraid.

"My worst fear," said Tina, "is that they'll throw me out in the street, or refuse to pay for college. Sometimes I don't know which would be worse." We all laughed, even though it wasn't at all funny.

"I've read about that happening sometimes, that a kid gets thrown out of the house," said Cynthia. "It's a real possibility."

"Yeah," Page added. "I guess everyone has to judge their situation for coming out based on who their parents are, too. I didn't think about the consequences much, just that I wanted to do it."

"Do you regret it?" I asked.

"No. Because I just couldn't live a lie anymore…But then again, if they'd thrown me out, maybe I would have wished I'd waited till I was on my own to tell them. I can't say. But it still feels upsetting that my dad slapped me and that they're acting like jerks now."

"And yet it's a relief that they know, right?" asked Cynthia gently.

"Yeah, it is. Even if they try to deny it, it's been said, they know, and they'll need to accept it eventually because I really am gay." She still seemed sad and a bit shaken.

"Do you think your dad would hit you again about it?" prodded Tina, reading my thoughts.

"Only if I push him on it. I've gotten advice to just give him space with it right now, not mention it for a while and just see what happens and if he'll accept it more. So that's what I think I'll do."

We all nodded and were quiet. Then to our surprise, Page started to cry. Cynthia moved her chair closer and put her arms around Page and held her.

We sat there, all realizing how hard coming out could be. And yet Cynthia had done it and gotten a better response and was happy with it, despite her being a bit pissed that they weren't thrilled. And even Page had said her parents knew who she was now, and so she didn't have to lie.

Were the benefits worth the risks for me? Coming out to my parents was something I was going to ponder for a while longer, but in my heart I knew I wanted to do it soon.

CHAPTER 28

I woke up whispering, "No! No! Leave me alone," though in my dream, I was shouting.

"Oh no, not another one," I thought. It was about 7:00 a.m. on Sunday. I lay there for a while thinking about it. Another coming out nightmare.

I hated not being able to tell my parents. I just *had* to tell them. God, I didn't even want to be thinking about all this on a Sunday morning, but there I was, mulling it over.

At least I was getting more determined to tell my parents I was gay. The question then became when. And how.

I wondered if I should I casually mention it at the dinner table? "What's new? Well, I got an A in history, I'm gay, and I saw a good movie last night. Pass the ketchup, please, Becky?"

Or I could leave a message on the answering machine. "Hi. This is Sarah. I'm staying late after school today, I'm gay, and I'll be home around seven."

I could even put it in my will and if I die early, they would read, "…Wishes to have her parents know she was gay." Or I could leave them a book under our Christmas tree this year, *Dealing With Your Child's Homosexuality*.

Ugh!, I thought. I am driving myself crazy!

Things seemed to snowball after that.

I was reading a novel the next week about a lesbian and her career on Wall Street. The cover looks perfectly normal so I hadn't even thought twice about reading it on the bus or in my room.

Then my mom said, "What are you reading, dear?"

"Oh, just a novel…for school." I hadn't even heard her come up the stairs until she'd knocked and poked her head in my half open door.

"Oh, well, dad says dinner will be ready in one minute. Can I see?" She motioned towards my book.

I started to sweat. "Oh, it's just a book about someone's life on Wall Street." I flashed the cover at her. "I'm really engrossed right now. I'll be right down for dinner."

"Oh. Okay." She seemed surprised and hurt that I wasn't telling her more. "See you down there," she said, and she left.

I was glad she hadn't pushed the issue, and yet I felt horrible. I couldn't even read a lesbian novel without worrying my parents would see it and maybe be more suspicious. My mom probably thought I was reading some dirty book or just that I was in a private mood and didn't want to tell her what I was doing. But I still didn't feel ready to tell them.

To add to everything, later that day, Becky motioned toward me when I passed the open door of her room.

"Hey, Sarah?"

"Yeah? What's up?" I said a bit too harshly, then I felt bad. I knew I was under pressure from a lot of things, not just hiding my sexuality: lots of work at school, Tina got pissed at me for something I said, and me just not getting enough sleep.

"I just wanted to ask if you're okay. You just seemed tense or something at dinner all week."

I stared at her for a second, then decided to be honest. I reminded myself that she already knew about me and Tina. "Yeah, I am tense." I sat down at her desk chair. "It's tests, sleep, Tina, me and Tina, not telling our folks…" I whispered the last few.

She nodded sympathetically.

"Do you think you'll tell them soon?" She didn't seem to be pressuring me, just caring. I really needed it at that moment.

"I don't know. I might. God knows I'd like to but when I try, my mouth just stays shut. What do you think I should do?" I laughed, but I really did want to hear what she had to say.

"I think you should tell them," she said outright.

It felt scary and yet good. "Really?"

"Yes. I think it's taking a lot out of you to not tell them, and it's hurting you and ultimately them. And they're not going to throw you out."

"Yeah, you're probably right." I thought about it. If I really asked myself, I knew it would ultimately be okay. "Okay, I'll tell them."

"Well, don't do it because I said so; it should be for you."

"I know, I know. I need to tell them and I will. When and how: that's what I'm wondering about."

"You'll find a way."

"Oh, you're no help."

She laughed. "Well, let me know when you do."

"Oh, you'll hear about it, one way or another." I said as I moved towards the door.

I waved and went to my room.

Thinking about it all, I realized I was as ready as I'd ever be to tell my parents. I vowed that at the first opportunity, I would do it.

CHAPTER 29

✿

I couldn't keep my promise to myself.

Now and then I'd have a good opening, dozens of them. "So what's new in your life, dear?" My mom would say. Or, "How's your love life?" Or, "Any interesting boys in your classes?," my dad would say. I always hesitated, but then I gave the same beating around the bush answers I always gave and still felt angry and held back.

Tina was really supportive, even though she had decided not to come out to her parents this year because she knew they were so conservative. They even made homophobic comments sometimes, so she had just decided not to tell them right now.

As for our relationship, it was going strong. For the holidays, she had even given me a silver ring with a heart in it. "A friendship ring" was what we called it.

It made me feel really sad to think about us being apart next year, since we'd probably be going to different colleges. Both of us were interested in schools with good programs in our main interests (Tina in art and me in ornithology), plus both of us wanted schools with active gay student organizations. So we could only wait and see where we each got in. One part of me felt glad we mostly hadn't applied to the same schools, since we were independent people with different interests. The main part of me, though, felt like I'd totally die without her! I really loved her so much, and it made me crazy to think of being hours away next year. So I mostly dealt with it by trying not to think about it much. After all, there was a whole lot of the school year left to enjoy, with plenty of both kisses and coming out challenges ahead of us.

I also had another dream sometime in January which helped me deal with telling (and not telling) my parents about us. In this dream, my grandmother came to me flying with wings like an angel, took my left hand in hers, and flew me off with her to sit on a cloud, looking down at Ithaca. I stared into grandma's eyes and she stared into mine, squeezing my hand. I could feel her wrinkled skin with my fingers, just as it had felt the last time I'd seen her in the nursing home, and I could smell her clothes smelling of the nursing home smell, comforting to me now. I said, "Grandma,…but you're dead!" She said, "Only on this earth. I just came to tell you I know all about you and Tina, and I love you, just as much as I ever did, and I'll never stop loving you. Always remember how much I love you." Then I cried and cried as she held me in her arms.

I woke up crying real tears, wanting her to be alive. She was dead, I knew she was, but maybe it was true that she would somehow always love me and that somehow her love could stay with me even in death.

I layed in the dark and thought about it a while, then I rolled over and went back to sleep. I knew then that somehow I'd tell my parents when the time was right.

CHAPTER 30

For Valentine's Day, I got Tina a friendship ring, too, and she got me a subscription to a national gay newspaper. To celebrate together, we went cross-country skiing in one of the local parks.

It was a crystal clear day and the sky was a beautiful blue. The snow was about a foot deep in the park, and since no one was around, we held hands when we felt like it.

"Are you getting nervous about hearing from the colleges?" Tina asked.

"You better believe it. Only two more months at the most and then we'll know!"

"I know. I'm worried, too."

I thought again about us being apart next year. I looked at her, and then looked away.

"What?" she asked.

"I guess I'm thinking how I'll miss you next year. I guess it's starting to sink in more."

"Aw." She took my hand again. "I know. I try not to think about it, but it's true."

We stopped walking for a minute.

"I love you." I kissed her on the mouth.

"And I love you, my dear madam."

We kissed again, for a long time. Her tongue felt warm in my mouth and we started to get hot and heavy. If it hadn't been twenty-five degrees out with twelve inches of snow on the ground, I'm sure we would have loved to have sex right there.

❀   ❀   ❀

Later that afternoon, after our skiing expedition, we went to Danny's Diner for some hot cocoa.

Jarod was there with his friend, Art. I chuckled to myself, wondering if he was the new crush that Jarod had been hinting about. They waved, and a few minutes later, they walked over on their way out.

"Hey Tina, hey Sarah dear." He kissed the top of my head. "How are you? I tried calling you this morning."

"Yeah, we were wilderness travelers today." I motioned in the direction of the skis.

"So I see. Art, you know Sarah and Tina, don't you?"

"Yeah, we're in the same economics class, right?" he said to Tina.

"Yeah, did you try the assignment yet? It's a killer."

"I'll bet. It looks it. I've been procrastinating about it all weekend."

"Well, feel free to call me if you need help. I'm in the phone book under Gerald Hawkins, my dad."

"Okay, maybe I will." He seemed grateful for the offer.

"All right, women. We don't want to keep interrupting," said Jarod. To me, he said, "We're still on for studying tomorrow, right?"

"Yup. It's a date. And you're never an interruption."

Jarod smiled. "Thanks, but we should scoot just the same. Ta." He blew Tina and me kisses, and then he and Art left.

Tina and I looked at each other.

I said, "I think Art has a crush on you."

"Art?" Tina eyes opened wide. "What makes you think so?"

"Well, I'd seen him looking at you in class several times. I don't know. It's just a feeling."

"If he only knew." She touched my hand briefly. "Well, if he calls, maybe I'll drop a hint."

"Like what?" I asked, giggling.

"Oh, like "Good timing. I just got done with a call from my girlfriend."

"Or you could say, 'the woman I'm in love with.'"

"Yeah. I wish I could just say it". She looked sad. "Well, I'm not going to worry about it."

"Mm", I said. I touched her hand for a second, then moved it away when I saw who was heading into the diner.

"So how's your English thesis going?"

We chatted, as Mindy came in with her two cronies, Brenda and Helen.

"Oh no, here comes trouble." Tina flicked her eyes in their direction and grimaced.

"Well, let's hope not," I said. But I sensed something didn't feel right in the air.

They were going to sit on the other side of the diner, then chose instead to sit at the booth next to us.

"Hi men," called Mindy. "How ya doing?"

I flinched at the way she called us men. What was her problem?

"Hi Mindy. How're *you* doing?," Tina responded calmly.

"Not bad. We just all went to the movies. How about you two? On a *date?*" She emphasized the last word.

I couldn't believe how she was hinting at us like that.

"We were cross-country skiing." Tina's voice was still amazingly calm; she looked calm, too. I however, felt my heart beating quick and my face getting hot.

Then Helen piped up and said, as if it were rehearsed, "Our movie was about a bunch of fags, 'La Cage Aux Folles II.' We—"

Tina stood up and said, "That's enough of harassment. You three all know we're gay and are a couple, so why don't you just grow up!" Her face was bright red and her fists were clenched. I'd never seen her so angry.

"Why don't you grow up, Hawkins," Mindy hollered back. "You'd come on to all of us if you could."

By now, everyone in the place was staring at us, and the manager was walking towards us looking angry.

"Well, I have a feeling you wouldn't mind."

Tina's comment obviously snapped something in Mindy, because she threw a quick punch at Tina's chin and then jumped into our booth and right onto Tina, trying to punch her lights out. Tina started fighting back, and then I tried to pull Mindy off. Before I knew it, Brenda and Helen were both on me holding and twisting my arms, and then we were all in a punching and kicking match.

They got me a few times in the face and chest; at least I had the satisfaction of getting in a few good kicks myself before the manager and someone else pulled us all apart. We were still all yelling at each other when I heard a police siren; I guess someone in the diner had called them.

Before I knew it, Tina and I had been thrown into a police car and Mindy, Brenda, and Helen into another. Tina and I just kind of collapsed in the seat. We were both sore and bleeding from a few scratches but nothing serious, thank god.

"Are you okay?" I put my hand on her shoulder.

She nodded. "I think I am. What about you?"

"Okay I guess." I gave her hand a quick squeeze and we held eye contact for a few seconds; other than that, we mostly tended to our own wounds until we got to the police station.

Luckily, there were a lot of rows of benches at the police station, so we didn't have to be near the other girls. The cop who drove our car said, "Okay, we've questioned the people at the diner; now we'll take each of you one by one. You're first," and he motioned me into another room.

It was pretty bare, with just a bunch of chairs, file cabinets, and a desk in the corner.

"Name?"

"Sarah Goldberg."

"Age?"

He asked me all that informational stuff and then finally, "Okay, what's the story?"

I told it to him as best I could.

When I was done, he said, "You know Sarah, you two need to avoid getting into fights with those girls. They sound like they're just looking for a fight, and your being gay, assuming that's what you are, is their excuse. Don't play into their taunts; you can walk away. And you know you're lucky you weren't gay-bashed earlier than this. I have a cousin who's gay, and he was beaten up all the time in high school."

I just kind of stared at him. I was still in shock from everything and glad he was being so open and supportive in his own way. Maybe because it was a pretty liberal town, the police officer seemed pretty liberal, too.

"How out are you two about being lesbians, anyway?"

"Well," I said, still surprised I was having this conversation with a police officer, "most people haven't been told, even most of our friends, but many have guessed. And I think those girls know more than most, because Tina used to hang out with one of them."

"Hmm. Well, I've got to admire your courage."

"Really?"

"Really. You have the right to be who you are and go to a diner or do anything you want. Just be careful, okay? And no more fights."

"Thanks. I'll definitely try." I just looked at him, shaken up by everything that had just happened. I cleared my throat. "So, what kind of trouble are we in? Will we have to stay in jail?"

He chuckled. "No, nothing that bad. All your parents will be called. And you each might have to do some work for the diner, to make up for disturbing the peace."

I gulped when I hear my parents were being called. "Will our parents be told what happened?"

"Just about the fight. You all can fill in the details. And the town paper might report it tomorrow: it was a slow weekend."

I cursed to myself. I didn't want this to be the way my parents found out.

The cop led me back to the big room, and Tina was called in next. We gave each other a quick look beforehand, and I tried to convey the message that it had been okay.

After they let Tina out, Mindy went in, and then Brenda and Helen were also called in at the same time. Throughout all this, we had stayed on our side of the room and the other girls had stayed on theirs. We hadn't really looked at each other.

Tina told me while we were waiting that the cop was going to reprimand the three of them about gay-bashing. I knew we'd really gotten lucky with this guy. A lot of cops might not be on our side so much (or on our side at all for that matter).

Tina told me the cop had reprimanded her, too, for getting into the argument. He said if we get taunted again, we should just walk away and not bother talking, for it could only escalate. Basically, it was what the cop had said to me. And we had to admit it was true. It's not always easy to walk away from a fight, but it was probably what we needed to do.

Then I said to Tina, "Despite all this, I don't regret one bit hanging out with you. We've got a right to go to the diner. And we didn't start that fight."

"I know," she said. "Mindy certainly has a lot of anger about *her* being called gay."

"Yeah." I I elbowed Tina and smiled. "Maybe she's jealous and wants your body."

"Yeah. Maybe." Tina raised her eyebrows at me. "But don't worry, I only want you."

Tina and I exchanged our special smile.

Soon the other girls got sent back to the waiting area. Then we heard an officer calling all of our parents in the next room, and I started sweating. Tina did, too, and we gave each other a look of, "Oh, no—now we *really* have to deal with our parents."

The next twenty minutes were interminable after the officer told us that both our parents would be down soon. I had no idea what would happen: I was imagining the worst, praying for the best. I watched them book some new guy who had come in handcuffed. I wondered if my own parents would think I was an outlaw.

We just sat and waited.

After a while, my folks came in, looking very upset and worried. Tina's parents were right behind them.

My parents came over.

"Sarah, are you all right?," my dad asked. He seemed a mixture of worried and angry, confused and surprised.

"Yeah, just a few scratches." I could see Tina getting the same surprised questioning from her folks.

The officer was waiting there to talk with them. My parent and Tina's filed into the office. Tina and I looked at each other, still nervous. "Well, we'll see what happens," I said.

"Yeah." She looked really scared, so I gave her one of our special pokes.

Then I figured: what the hell, everyone here knows we're gay anyway, so I gave her hand a quick squeeze.

She looked tenderly into my eyes. "We're in this together," she said.

"I know, and I'm glad it's with you."

Then we waited for what seemed like hours, but when they came out of the office, it had really only been five minutes. The parents of the other three girls weren't there yet.

I saw my dad shaking the officer's hand and thanking him. I saw my parents give Mindy and her friends a dirty look, then come over towards me. "Okay, Sarah. Let's go home." Dad stretched out his hand, and I took it.

I got up to go. "I'll talk to you later, Tina."

"Okay." She looked scared as her parents came towards her. They seemed worried and quiet, too. I went with my parents out to the car, and we walked the whole way in silence.

CHAPTER 31

My parents looked at me and then at each other. I wasn't sure what to say. We got into the car and all sat there.

Mom broke the silence. "Well, we're not too angry, Sarah. I just hope you and Tina won't be getting into any more fist fights. I just don't want you to get hurt."

"Thanks. I hope I don't either."

We both paused.

"Do you want to say anything more about it?" dad asked.

"Well, just that I guess we should have left when they came into the diner and started bothering us. I wish we hadn't gotten into the fight with them."

"Yes, that sounds like a good idea for the future."

"So did the police tell you, uh,…what it was about?"

"No, they just said it was some taunting and insults among teenagers."

Stomach did flip-flops. So they didn't know, and I wouldn't have to tell them.

But do it, I told myself. Do it.

"Well," I said. "It was about something. They were taunting us about…about Tina and me being gay."

There was a pause of about five seconds which seemed more like five hours. My heart was racing: this was the real thing. I was coming out to my parents.

"Are you?" dad asked.

"Yes," I said, looking him squarely in the eye, then at mom. "We are. We're a couple."

"Wow," said mom. "I've been wondering for some time."

"You have?" Even though I'd half hoped she'd suspected, still it felt weird to know she really had seriously been wondering about me. "What tipped you off?"

"I guess just that you were always with Tina, you brought her to grandma's funeral, and you'd never expressed any real interest in boys. We weren't sure or anything, we'd just suspected." Mom took my hand. "And honey, it doesn't change how we feel about you."

Tears came to my eyes.

"I agree," said dad. "We love you and want you to be happy. I mean, I wish you liked boys, but I want to accept you, and I definitely love you no matter what. We can talk more about it later. Just be careful, meaning don't get into anything where we have to pick you up at the police station again." He scrunched up his forehead and took my other hand.

"Thanks." I practically choked on my words, and I started to cry. "I've been wanting to tell you two for a long time, but I was scared you'd hate me or something."

"Oh Sarah," said dad. "We'd never hate you. Like I said, it does take a bit of getting used to, even if your mom suspected, but it's okay. Really. You're still Sarah. I love you"

"And I love you, Sarah," said mom.

"I love you, too," I said to both of them, still crying. I looked at them and squeezed their hands.

Mom hugged me across the seats, then added with a smile, "But does this mean you won't be giving us any grandchildren?"

I laughed and dried my eyes. "Oh mom. How can I know? I mean, sure, it does seem less likely, since I'm a woman who falls in love with women, but I might like to have kids. So maybe I'll decide to get inseminated by a sperm donor."

"That's true, you could do that," said mom, thinking it over. "Well, it doesn't matter for now. I'm just really glad you weren't hurt today, and I'm glad you finally told us about…your preference. I wish it didn't have to come from being arrested, but in any case, it's done."

"Yeah. And I'm really glad you both finally know." I reached forward and hugged the two of them from behind, as best I could in the small car.

And I breathed one of the biggest sighs of relief in my life.

CHAPTER 32

The school year rolled on.

The story had made the papers, and it mentioned all of our names, but it didn't directly state what the fight was about. Everyone in the high school knew, though; word gets around. Occasionally, some students we didn't know gave us a few strange looks, but only Mindy and her friends would say anything. Sometimes they'd spit, but as with the verbal baits, we were just walking away for now and reporting it to the Dean. I know he called them in to talk once or twice but I don't know if it helped. Another time, I caught Mr. Vantam staring at us with a frown in the hallway, and I could have sworn I'd heard him whisper "Lesbians" under his breath. My heart sank, because I'd always liked him and trusted him.

As for our friends, they were cool with the news. Some had suspected, some hadn't, but most of them stuck with us. One friend, Libby, did stop calling me to do stuff, which hurt. Then I figured it was her hang-up, and I gave her space. I wasn't real close with her to begin with, so it wasn't a huge deal, but it felt weird. At some level, I know I really did feel awful about it, as she also represented all the other people I was afraid of losing.

Overall, I knew that Tina and I were a lot luckier than many gay teens with the reactions we were getting, which made it easier to ignore Mindy and company. But, again, it hurt. All the homophobia hurt.

As for Tina's parents, they never mentioned or talked about her being gay, after Tina, like me, had decided to tell them after the fight. Tina tried to get them to talk about their feelings, but they said outright that they didn't want to talk about it. That made me feel lucky with my parents, and I felt really sad for Tina.

Jarod was thinking of coming out more openly, too. He had a boyfriend now, Craig from the coming out group, who he'd finally met in gym class. We went on some double dates and even a triple date once with Page and Cynthia. It felt great to really know other gay couples.

On other fronts, we'd heard from the colleges. I would be going to the University of Massachusetts at Amherst, and Tina would be going to Wellesley College. Though I was sad we'd be apart, at least we'd be within a few hours of each other so we'd be able to visit pretty easily. And Jarod would be at Hampshire College, which was nearby to Amherst, so I was glad about that, too.

It was definitely depressing, though, to think of being apart from Tina next year. I knew it might "be good for me," because I would find out more of who I was without her, but it made me just want to cry and hold her and never let go. But I knew I'd have to let go, come late August, so for now, I just tried to enjoy the months we had left together.

The biggest excitement was looking forward to the senior prom. I couldn't wait! It would be me, Tina, Jarod, Craig, Page and Cynthia (we found out we were allowed to invite friends from outside of our high school), plus a lot of our straight friends would be there, too: Freida, Gus, Abdul, and Sylvia. I thought of how far Tina and I had come since last June's dance. Just last spring I was thinking I'd always be single and that there were probably no other lesbian girls around, and now I'd been with Tina almost ten months! Plus I had many gay friends and acquaintances, thanks to the support group and to Jarod.

It felt great looking forward to having Tina as my real date this year for the dance. I just hoped that people like Mindy wouldn't give us any more trouble.

CHAPTER 33

Our group had decided to gather at Jarod's place, since we wanted to all hang out a bit before the dance. Then the limo could just pick us up from there.

As I walked over, I thought of grandma. A year ago, she'd called me to wish me luck at the junior dance, and now she was dead! It made me want to jump up and down and throw a tantrum, but I also thought of the dream I'd had of grandma and her loving me always. That made me feel stronger to face being an "out" lesbian at the dance with my lover, Tina.

I got to Jarod's place early, and he and I gave each other a big hug.

"I'm really glad we'll all be at the dance again together," he said. "And I'm glad you're my friend." Then he kissed my cheek.

"Aw, thanks Jarod. Me, too. I don't know what I would have done without your support through my coming out stuff."

"No problem. And it makes it easier for me now that I'm coming out more, too."

"Really?"

"Yeah. Helping you made me have to live my own advice."

"Great. So how 'out there' do you think you and Craig will be tonight?"

"You mean how obvious?"

"Well, Tina and I talked about it a lot. We finally figured we'd dance a slow dance or two, and play it by ear about how physically affectionate to be."

"That's great. I'll ask Craig when he gets here. I think it's harder for guys, because girls can get away with more physical affection."

"Yeah, you might be right," I said. "It's still a huge risk, though, to dance a slow dance with another girl. It's not exactly the usual thing at this school".

"That's true. You and Tina have already gotten your share of harassment, what with the diner thing and getting spit on and everything. It pisses me off."

"Yeah, we've certainly been harassed."

"But you know, I'm willing to risk it tonight. What the hell? We'll all only be at this dumb school another three weeks."

"Yeah, and how much could they to do to you and Craig, or to Tina and me? There are all those teacher chaperones, so if they do jump you or something, they won't really hurt you."

"I hope." He looked at me seriously.

"That's true." We'd both read enough articles in the national gay paper about anti-gay violence.

The doorbell rang then and the others began arriving. When Tina got there, I gave her a big kiss on the lips and we hugged; no one batted an eye, which felt really nice. I felt grateful for all my wonderful friends.

I talked more with Tina about PDA's (Public Displays of Affection). We decided that despite the risks, we'd definitely do it.

I asked Page and Cynthia what they were going to do. We all agreed there was safety in numbers and that it couldn't hurt; we had nothing to be ashamed of. We also agreed that if anyone taunted us, we'd ignore them and walk away, approach some of the teacher chaperones or call the police. After all, we deserved to enjoy the dance without any verbal abuse. In any case, we wouldn't play into any antagonism, and we mainly hoped it would just be a totally fun night.

I definitely felt good about feeling free to show my affection for Tina. On the other hand, I was scared of what might happen. It was a risk I was willing to take; I felt tired, really tired, of hiding who I was. My parents had been a big hurdle, and now here was the school dance again. I knew at least that Tina and I were known to be gay, but if I couldn't be outwardly gay at our school dance, what would be the point of going? And what was the point of coming out?

And at this year's dance, I knew I wasn't going it alone.

CHAPTER 34

The gym was already crowded when we got there. The decorations, in glimmering purple, green, and silver, hung about everywhere, and along with the flashing disco lights in the dark, they really made the place festive.

I looked at Tina and, for the first time, publicly squeezed her hand. Granted, we let go after only ten seconds, but it felt good. No one killed us; the world didn't end. We were coming out!

The school had a great new DJ this year. We all ran out on the dance floor pretty quickly and began jumping and swinging to the fast music. It felt so great. And I'm sure it wasn't just the music. Our group was so much closer this year, and we also knew we'd all be going our separate ways in the fall.

My heart started beating crazily when I thought about us planning to be to be really "out" tonight. What if someone did try to hurt us? And yet I still wanted to be out, and I was proud of both my gay and straight friends.

We all danced in a big circle for a while, so nothing was obvious at first. Sometimes we all joined hands and made a big circle, swinging each other around. We were definitely not a "boy-girl-boy-girl" circle. It just felt great; I really loved the dancing.

Then we took a break for a while, and I stood with Tina. We smiled, and again we held hands.

"Having a good time?" she asked.

I noticed a few stares but I just ignored them. "The best," I said, looking at her. "This is a lot better than last year, huh?"

"Uh hmm. So are we going to slow dance?" She stood close to me and kissed my cheek.

"I think so." I giggled, sounding like Becky. "My knees are still shaking, but I want to."

"I'm scared, too. At least we won't be alone tonight." She motioned her eyes in the direction of Cynthia and Page, who were jitterbugging together. They weren't obvious yet; girls do that all the time, but we knew it was different.

"We could try that jitterbugging," I said, taking her two hands in mine and smiling at her.

"What? You mean all those fancy steps?"

Jarod interrupted. "Hey you two. So are you going to get out there and show some togetherness?"

Tina and I looked at each other and laughed.

"You read our minds," Tina said. "We were just thinking of copying Cynthia and Page. Will you and Craig do it, too?"

'Well, I have two left feet. I'd have hoped my gay debut would be more impressive for my dancing abilities, but this will do. Hey, Craig." He waved him over from where he was chatting with Abdul.

Craig finished his conversation and skipped over to us. "Yes, my love?"

"Tina and Sarah are suggesting we couples go jitterbug, or try to, anyway. Are you game?"

"Ready as I'll ever be, I suppose." He looked more serious now, and he looked at all of us. I could tell he was nervous, too. "Shall we?" He extended an elbow to Jarod.

"Let's."

They moved towards Cynthia and Page as Tina and I watched. Then Jarod whispered something in Craig's ear, and they ran back and grabbed our wrists.

"Come on you two: it was your idea."

"Okay, okay," I said.

Again, I felt like I'd have a heart attack as we moved onto the dance floor. We were coming out, advanced level.

CHAPTER 35

I tried to focus my attention totally on the dancing; it wasn't easy, but I came close. We tried to do just what Cynthia and Page were doing.

"Move your feet like this," Page said. We tried to follow along. It was kind of fun. In fact I liked it a lot. Jarod and Craig seemed to be enjoying it, too.

Of course, I was very aware of some stares that we were getting, even though I tried to pretend that I didn't notice. People would stare, then go back to their own dancing. Or they'd stand in a crowd and giggle, but then they seemed to lose interest.

We went back to regular fast "disco" style dancing for the next few dances, dancing as a group. It was good to take a break from being so out. It definitely felt nerve wracking.

"How're you doing, partner?," Tina asked at one point, elbowing me.

"Okay," I said, elbowing back. "Still quaking in my boots. But basically, I'm all right. You?"

"The same. I think I can get used to it, though. As long as they don't harass us, I'm glad we're acting like a couple."

"Good."

"But you know, if you ever get too nervous, we can take a break or stop. We have to both want to do it."

"Thanks." I felt relieved. "That's nice to hear. But for now, I still want to dance together. You're my girlfriend after all."

"Thank you, ma'am."

"But if I start freaking out, I'll tell you."

"Good."

"And the same for you. If you freak out, I want you to tell me, too."

"I will…"

A slow dance came on. We went out on the dance floor and swayed together. I could see Page and Cynthia nearby, too.

Tina smiled. "Can I kiss you?"

I was filled with love and my heart and belly did a flip-flop. It overrode my feeling of nervousness as to what people would think. I nodded.

She leaned over and kissed me, and we kissed a long kiss, about ten seconds. I felt her sweet, salty lips on mine, and she felt warm as we pressed together. Our tongues danced around briefly and we stood close. Then we detached, smiled, and danced towards Cynthia and Page to see how they were doing.

Page whistled at us and said, "Hey, kids, I couldn't help noticing you two challenging the heterosexist system tonight."

I blushed. Tina did, too. But I didn't mind their teasing.

"Yeah," continued Cynthia. "You're an example for all of us."

"Aw, it was nothing." I smiled at Tina. "Just true love at work."

"That's right my love," said Tina. "True love, and a lot of courage on all our parts."

We all nodded. It felt so good to be out and be with gay friends.

Then I heard Bruce shout, "Dykes! Queers!"

Tina and I looked at each other. I didn't know whether to ignore them or turn and look at them or what. God knows I wanted to yell something right back to them.

I really didn't know what to do, but then Tina and Cynthia turned to face them and so I did, too. There was Bruce and a pack of about five guys walking by and staring at us, laughing and pointing. I felt a mixture of shock, fear, anger, and disgust. I looked at Tina and Cynthia again. Together, we all just looked at the guys. We kept out shoulders back and our heads up, showing our dignity.

The guys kept walking by and went away, and the moment passed.

We all relaxed and looked at each other. "Well," said Page. "Shall we all dance some more?"

It seemed like more than I could handle.

"I think I'll sit this one out." I needed a chance to get calm again.

"I will, too," said Tina. "Come on, honey." She took my hand and we headed back to where Jarod, Craig, Freida, Gus and some of the others were sitting.

"Sorry," I said softly to Tina. "I needed a break."

"It's fine," said Tina. "I needed a break, too. In fact I'm glad you said it. I might have kept dancing anyway, wanting to appear tough to Cynthia and Page or something. But I guess they'll be okay."

Jarod came right over to us. "Those guys were real jerks out there." He pounded his fist into his palm. "I'm glad they finally left you alone," he added.

"Me too." I must have looked really worried because Jarod squeezed my hand. I took a deep breath.

"How about you, Jarod? Did you all have any problems with anyone yet tonight?"

Jarod nodded his head. "A few snide comments and some stares. But it's none too pleasant, as you know, and we deserve not to be stared at at all. I—"

"Hey, it's homo city." I looked up to see Mindy swagger by with Brenda. We all ignored them and tried to keep talking.

"So, uh, Jarod, what did you think of the physics test?"

"Not bad. Mr. Marting made it pretty easy."

"Hey you fags and dykes. Yoo hoo." She waved and walked by again.

We did a pretty good job of keeping calm and pretending to be into our conversation, but our tension level was rising, and I thought my blood pressure must be sky high.

Mindy and Brenda sauntered off again, much to my relief.

"God, what is her problem?," asked Tina. "I wish I could break her face off."

I nodded. "I know, I know. And probably nothing can change her."

"It really scares me, too," said Jarod. "I'm angry, but I also don't want anyone beating us up or anything."

"I know," said Craig. "I probably shouldn't read all those articles about gay bashings, but they are a reality…."

"Should we tell one of the chaperones, do you think?," Tina asked me.

"I don't know. I guess we should—that was our plan." I thought about it. "I wonder if some of the chaperones are just ignoring the taunts, like Mr. Vantam, but maybe Mr. Marting and Ms Schwartz didn't even hear them. But if we did tell them, how do you all think they'd react?" I leaned over and looked at Page and Cynthia.

"Well, there's one way to find out," said Page. "I'm going. Anyone coming with me?" She looked at all of us.

I glanced over at Mr. Marting, the physics teacher. Tell *him* we're being verbally harassed for being gay? Well, rumors had been all over the school after the scene in the diner. Who was I to think he hadn't heard about it like most people? Anyway, we deserved protection, I reminded myself.

"I will," I gulped. "That's what they're here for: to make sure we're all safe. Let's go."

Tina squeezed my hand, and Page and I went.

"Mr. Marting?" she said.

"Yes? Your name is…?" he said in a friendly way.

"I'm Page, a friend of Sarah's here."

"Nice to meet you. And hello, Sarah. Are you two enjoying yourselves?"

"Well, yes and no." I laughed nervously.

"Actually," said Page, "we want to report some harassment from some of the other kids here."

Mr. Marting looked confused and concerned. "Harassment? Here? By whom?"

I took a deep breath. "Mindy, Brenda, Helen, and that crowd. Also Bruce and his friends."

"I see." He glanced around and tried to spot them. "Do you know if anything started it?"

Here goes, I thought.

"Well, yes," I said. "They've been calling us gay and queer and fags and dykes, Mr. Marting. Because, to tell you the truth, a bunch of us are, and we haven't been hiding it tonight. Perhaps you've noticed it yourself."

His face turned red. "No, I haven't," he stammered. "Well, hmm. Well, good for you and your friends for being 'out'. I did hear a rumor about some gay-related scuffle you were involved in, Sarah. But I'm concerned about tonight."

I found myself breathing easier as it became clear that he was being supportive, even if he was nervous.

He continued, "I don't want any fights here or anyone getting hurt."

Page and I looked at each other.

"Neither do we," she said.

"Well, let's brainstorm what we can do tonight to prevent any further happenings," Mr. Marting said, running his hands through his beard. "Maybe if we also spoke with Ms. Schwartz and Mr. Vantam, so it wouldn't just—"

Just then we were cut off by the sound of loud voices back in the area where our group had been congregating most of the night.

I saw Mindy, Brenda, and Helen, as well as Bruce and his friends, crowded around near Tina, Cynthia, Jarod, Craig, and our other friends.

"Oh no!", I said, and I ran over there. Page and Mr. Marting were close at my heels, and I saw Ms. Schwartz running over, too.

"Dykes! Who do you think you are flaunting yourselves here?" Mindy was yelling.

I ran over and stood near Tina. She looked as relieved as hell to see me.

There was still some space between the two groups, which was a good sign.

"Whoa," said Mr. Marting. "What's going on here?"

They ignored him.

"I said what's going on here?" he said louder.

Mindy looked at him. "They have no right being here and flaunting their sexuality like that. Stupid queers!" She stepped closer to us, looking like she wanted a fight.

"Why don't we just break this up right now," Mr. Marting said.

"Yes. Let's live and let live," said Ms. Schwartz, who looked steaming mad with her face all red. Her hands were on her hips; I was surprised how big her muscles looked for such a small woman.

"No, you get out of the way," said Mindy, and she flicked open a knife.

My heart went cold. A gasp went up from the crowd.

"Hey, let's split. This isn't worth it," said Tina.

"Now Mindy, let's just put down the knife. They're being gay, however you might feel about it, is not worth anyone getting hurt or you getting expelled or imprisoned." Ms. Schwartz was calm; I admired her for it, scared as I was.

Somehow her voice had the effect of putting everything in slow motion, of stopping Mindy in her tracks. She looked hesitant for the first time.

I felt frozen. Jarod, Tina and all of our friends started moving slowly backwards. Tina pulled at my sleeve.

"Sarah, let's go." I started to step backwards and kept my eyes on Mindy, Brenda and crowd. I was scared they would lunge after us, cutting, at any second, and yet I wanted to lunge at them for trying to get us to leave.

Then a sound arose from where other kids were watching from a safe distance.

"Just leave them alone." Someone cried out. It was hard to tell who'd said it.

"Let them come back—they have a right to stay and dance!"

"They have the right to be gay!" another girl yelled.

"Stop bullying them."

"Having a knife doesn't make you tough!'

"Don't be a jerk: leave them alone!" some guy shouted.

That got Mindy's attention. "Who the hell said that?" she yelled. The knife was at her side again.

Then the crowd started chanting, "Leave them alone! Leave them alone!"

It was amazing! The whole gym was rocking with their voices.

"Leave them alone! LEAVE THEM ALONE!"

Brenda and Mindy looked at the crowd, looked back at their friends, shrugged, and they and their other friends backed off.

They all left, the crowd cheered, and Mr. Marting went to go call the police.

I was never more relieved in my life.

CHAPTER 36

We were all in shock and just stood there looking at each other, at all the other students, and at the door which had shut behind Mindy, Brenda, Helen, Bruce, and his friends. After a minute, we gradually started squeezing each others hands, and Ms. Schwartz and students we didn't even know came over and asked if we were okay or if there was anything they could do.

We heard some police sirens outside. Soon, a police officer came in and told us that they had picked up Mindy and company, and I was glad.

We all danced the last slow dance with our respective partners, and everyone applauded and whistled. It was wonderful: a dream come true. I just wished it hadn't taken near violence to get our schoolmates to respect and openly support us.

Our crowd left soon after to go to Jarod's house. We ran and laughed in the parking lot when we first got out, then came together and all just looked at each other.

"So, old Mindy and crowd are down at the police station again," I said.

"Yeah, I'm glad it's not us, and that we're not in an ambulance either," said Tina.

"You're telling me!" said Page.

'Could anyone go for a group hug?" piped up Freida. "I sure could use one."

"Sure, that's a great idea," I said, and everyone else agreed.

We all gathered in a circle and hugged. We stayed like that for several minutes, and we'd giggle when someone would walk by and had to go around us. We must have looked like we were in a football huddle.

We stayed quiet, and after a minute, Freida said quietly, "I was never so scared in my life!"

"Me either," said Tina. "I thought I'd pee in my pants."

None of us laughed, because we'd all been just as afraid.

"I was scared she'd cut one of us, when I saw her knife," I shared, practically whispering.

"Yeah, I'm glad we're all okay," said Page.

Everyone agreed and we all hugged each other a little tighter. After staying in our huddle a minute longer, Jarod said, "Here's to good friends."

"Here's to good friends!" we repeated, then separated and got back into the limo.

When we got to Jarod's house, we decided to call the police to see what had happened to Mindy. We weren't sure if we needed to press charges, because we figured the school would definitely do it.

The policeman said Mindy was in jail but would probably get bailed out by her folks. The school would bring the case to court, and the juvenile court system would take it from there. The officer on the phone also commended us for not escalating the fight, which felt good.

It had been a long night, so most of us headed home pretty soon.

I hugged Jarod good night. "Hey friend. I"m glad we're all okay."

"Me too," he said.

We smiled warmly at each other.

"I'll talk to you tomorrow," I said. "And maybe we can do the gorge this weekend?"

"You bet. We can work on our tans." He smiled and waved goodbye, and I said goodbye to the others. Tina and I walked home.

It was a dark night and late, around 1 a.m., so we held hands.

"Tonight was a lot different than last year's dance," Tina commented, squeezing my hand.

I put my arm around her waist. "I was really scared when I saw her coming at you with that knife." We stopped for a minute and I buried my face in her neck. Even though I was upset, it felt good to realize how much I loved the scent of her skin.

She kissed my cheek and held me tight. "I was scared, too, and I felt better when you ran over to me even if I was afraid you'd get hurt, too."

I nodded that I understood.

We looked at each other, then stood and held each other again. We looked into each other's eyes and kissed. My heart was dancing its usual flip-flops.

After a minute, I rested my head on her shoulder and said, "I don't even want to think about what could have happened. Or even about us going to different colleges soon. I don't ever want to lose you."

"Me either."

We kissed again, another long soft kiss, and pressed our bodies together.

Some cars drove by then, and we walked on. "I guess even a straight couple might not make out on the street with tons of cars going by," I mused.

"True, but it still bugs me that because we're lesbians, we have to feel more restricted," said Tina.

"Yeah, well we've done enough 'being out' work for one night."

"And you know what, Sarah?" she said. "The more I think back on when I was friends with Mindy, the more I feel like she was probably attracted to girls but just couldn't deal with that part of herself."

"That would definitely explain a lot."

We were both quiet for a minute, pondering that possibility.

Then I looked at her and smiled. "Well, I'm totally glad *we* can deal with it and that we're not hiding it anymore."

"That's for sure," she said. "And hopefully, some day it won't be an issue at all: we could all just be free to be ourselves."

"You said it!"

And we kissed once again, to consecrate our vision.

CHAPTER 37

❀

And so the school year ended with that excitement of our first planned public display of affection, our first conscious act of being publicly out, and its resulting backlash of fear, anger, and threats.

None of us regretted it, though. Most of our high school peers rose to the occasion in the next two weeks, smiling and saying hi, asking us if we were okay, saying they were glad we were out. Tons of people came up to us and offered support. And the student council put up signs in the halls that week saying "Safety and acceptance for all of our students."

Mindy got expelled and sent through the juvenile court and social services system. She wasn't allowed to come back to school for the last week of classes, but she did get her diploma, I heard.

We graduated in a sea of black hats and tassels flying through the air, and we all got together often, in groups and in pairs, to hang out in our last summer before going our separate ways. The gorge was a popular meeting spot, as always, and it was a glorious summer.

I still thought of grandma sometimes and felt sad, but more and more, the memory of her just made me feel happy and full of love. I still wished she hadn't died, of course, but I felt like the love she'd given me when she was alive was definitely with me. Her love was something growing in me all the time, becoming a type of self-love. When I thought of grandma now, it was like a motor propelling me to do what made me happy in life, like to study birds and to be an out lesbian.

And I was becoming more and more comfortable with my sexuality, with being a lesbian, with being "out." Even if some people didn't like it, I figured they had to accept it.

Tina and I were going strong. We'd settled into a quiet, loving acceptance of each other, very gentle and trusting. We had a "romantic bliss" that came from knowing we'd soon part.

We went all over the area that summer: hiking the state parks, going to movies and the gorge, and occasionally borrowing my parents' car and driving to outlying towns to explore or hear music.

We even made it to Provincetown for a long weekend with Page and Cynthia, getting a ride with a gay man from one of the colleges whose name we got off the bulletin board at Jack's Bar. We stayed in an all-women's Bed and Breakfast. It was a fantastic weekend: We went dancing in not just one, but several gay dance spots, went shopping, and went to the lesbian beach: It was incredible!

And Tina and I made love in our own little Bed and Breakfast room, without needing to hide, without needing to be scared, without needing to be ashamed. And that was truly something.

"You know," she said, "I'm really going to miss you, and miss us. It might not be the same after we start college." She stroked my cheek, looked into my eyes, and nibbled on my nose.

"Umm…," I mumbled. I felt reluctant to admit it, to keep acknowledging it. "It's hard to believe we're about to really start college, to be apart. It seems like just yesterday that we became friends. And just yesterday that I was eight, and I KNEW, but I couldn't tell anyone."

"Aw." She kissed my hair, my eyes, my lips. "You've known since you were eight. And now we both know."

We laughed, and I kissed her back.

And I truly *was* glad I've known since I was eight. You know?

-The End-

About the Author

Sophie Glasser wrote this young adult novel in spiral notebooks during her lunch hours at a boring job in 1990. She grew up in Bayside, Queens, New York, went to Stuyvesant High School in Manhattan, and attended Cornell University in Ithaca, New York, majoring in psychology as well as pursuing a concentration in women's studies. In her 20's, she pursued many creative interests, including writing fiction, poetry, and children's music. She also created awesome fabric painting (she is especially famous in her social circles for her hand-painted socks). In her 30's, she enrolled in Lesley University's "Creative Arts in Learning and Elementary Education" program in Cambridge, Massachusetts and received her master's degree. In addition to teaching in the elementary grades, she has taken to being a professional clown, and she loves bringing joy to children. She lives with her partner and cat in Somerville, Massachusetts, and she enjoys bird-watching.

0-595-29333-6

Printed in the United States
203064BV00004B/28-45/A